**"If you're telling the truth, you better go get it all
back, because you can't stay here." Kat needed
him to go before he discovered Lilly.**

"Time to change your plans, darlin.' We're in this together, and
I'm counting on you to pony up." Jake popped to his feet and
casually climbed toward her. "I'll do whatever it takes to keep
you."

She grabbed the screen door as a barricade. "It's too late for us,
Jake. Go get your job back. My life is the ranch. Yours is the
rodeo."

He covered the last two steps in a leap and slipped under her arm
that was gripping the door. He kissed her. She meant to resist, but
Jake's heat had always drawn her—a sensual bliss she'd once
feared to live without.

Their lips met with a sizzle that sparked through her. Kat felt a
soft moan of surrender escape. When he stepped back, Kat
loosened her hold on his neck. Her heart felt like it would pound
through her sleeveless flannel.

"I don't know, honey, I think you still like me." Jake flashed her a
cocky grin. "Can I stay?"

"Toad..." Kat growled. She loosened her fists when she realized
her short nails were scoring her palms. The man had skills. Staying
calm was key because he'd win if she got angry. He had to go. And
keep their rocky marriage afloat.

"No, Jake, you can't stay here. There's nothing for you in this
town. Don't pester me with questions. Let it go."

"Nope." He backed away from her, down the path, glancing at the
flowers she'd planted last year beside the cracked sidewalk. "Sorry
to break it to you, gorgeous, but I'm not going anywhere. Looks
like you're stuck with me," he declared. "Honey, I'm home!"

Keeping Kat

Riverbend Falls ~ Book 3

Delilah Dewey

ISBN: 979-8-9873319-4-1 (Paperback)
Library of Congress Control Number: 2023917687

KEEPING KAT

Printed on Demand in the United States of America.

First printing, 2023.

Delilah's Diction
adelilah@delilahsdiction.com

www.delilahsdiction.com

Dedication

To those of You who believed in me all along,
I know You. I love You.
Thank You!

Wow. What a ride! Friends who have given me a boost or sent positive vibes have filled my life, and I'm grateful. Thank you for being you!

Thank you to all the writers, readers, and bookstore owners who have shared their experiences or taken a chance on me. You've helped me grow in my craft.

I'm grateful to those who achieved success and shared their strategies. Thanks to ProWritingAid and Canva, my work looks top-notch.

To my street team, you rock! I love you guys! A special shout out for my beta readers. Your thoughtful insights helped shape the ultimate design of Riverbend Falls.

Kimber, you're a rockstar! You took my draft and helped me see the story I couldn't wait to read. Priceless.

A Super Duper thanks to my own hero, Sonny. You're my rock, and without your unwavering help and encouragement, I wouldn't be rolling.

Thanks to all my family for tolerating my wild notions, quiet moments, and scattered notes. Thank you for loving me despite my writing/reading obsessions and understanding that some writers are simply weird, and we love it. You're awesome! I love each one of you. Thanks for loving me just the way I am!

Chapter 1

"Cripes, that's all I need," Kat muttered to herself. A motorcycle echoed through the valley as it sped toward Kat's ranch, and she could see dust devils churning up in its wake. Whinnying and pounding hooves erupted from the corral behind her.

With a grunt of satisfaction for a job well done, she tossed the final square bale into position, then brushed the hay off her forearms and jeans. She'd long ago toughened her hide enough the scratchy texture of hay didn't bother her, so she decided she was good enough for an impromptu interview.

She tugged a piece of grass out of her dark ponytail and admired the full hay bay. Stacked right and tight. Tucking her gloves in her back pocket, she hitched the tailgate up on her trusty dusty Ford.

"Well, Dream, let's see what's behind door number one?" Kat patted her favorite horse on the neck as she walked by.

She assumed this dude was looking to fill the job she'd posted, but coming in hot on a bike to a horse sanctuary when job hunting wasn't overly bright. She was desperate enough to hear him out, anyway.

As she stepped into the early afternoon sunlight to calm her horses, the bike turned up her drive. She could have him come back. She hated the business of hiring and firing, but Grandpa Eli was out riding fence this morning and they needed a cowboy.

The dust settled, and she saw her husband, the famous Jake

Summers, straddling the bike, taking in his surroundings. The sight of him rooted her feet to the ground despite a compelling urge to duck back into the barn and hide.

She had too much going on to waste time arguing with him. Dust motes and hay chaff filled the air between them, and Kat wished it was a wall. She backed up in the barn's shadow and tried to figure out what to do. She wasn't ready for him, and she was so right about him riding in hot.

Despite being easy to look at, she sensed his temper was hot, too. Jake was rocking the dusty cotton, denim, and leather combo, but his lean, muscular shoulders were taut with frustration. He got off the machine and pulled a ragged ball cap from his back pocket, tugging it down over aviators that were already hiding his eyes.

He glimpsed her movement and threw up a half wave before charging the barn like an angry bull. His shoulders were squared, and his long legs propelled him forward, consuming the space between them. Kat knew he was itching for a brawl.

"What's the matter with you, woman?" He tugged his shades off and threw them on a barrel outside the barn door. He glanced down the drive bay of the barn, assuring they were alone, except for horses, then he glared at her.

Why didn't she take the lawyer's suggestion and mail the papers?

Well, that hadn't been Tom's advice exactly... he suggested Kat try counseling before doing anything rash. As if she were the hotheaded one!

Rash was eloping with Jake Summers over a decade ago. He was still the same impulsive, irresponsible guy sewed up in one irresistible package. A man she couldn't help but love. For what that was worth. She couldn't have picked a worse time to ask for a divorce.

Could she bluff her way out of this?

"Hey there, handsome. Fancy meeting you here. What brings you to the Ozarks?"

He was close enough now she could see deep tired lines on his face. When she met him in Amarillo six weeks ago, he was his usual sunny self, but now Jake looked tired and dark hollows had settled under his Caribbean blue eyes. The storm that darkened their depths promised he was going to be hard to wrangle around this time.

"Don't play games with me, Kat."

He tugged at his hat brim, then pulled it off, and she knew his temper was close to breaking by the way he dragged his hand through his caramel curls. She should have found some way to defuse her actions. Kat had weeks to call—or text, at least.

She had hoped he would neglect the paperwork until it suited him, and she could figure out how to settle Lilly without involving him. She didn't have it all figured out yet, but he was here. Maybe...

"Why'd you have to play with my heart and leave me with divorce papers? How could you be so cold?" He shook his head and grabbed his shades. "You didn't even say anything was wrong. It's maddening."

"What I had in mind was—well, I wasn't looking to start an argument, then or now. I came to say goodbye, but... we've talked it to death. You don't want to quit the circuit and I've outgrown my taste for it. Our lives have been going in different directions for a while... I thought it was time to stop torturing ourselves."

Honestly, she just wanted to stop torturing herself.

She still watched the rodeos online, despite not wanting to see him hurt, and she could see buckle bunnies drifting along beside him in every town.

She believed him he hadn't strayed—he was so single-minded since the accident—but he *could*. Kat tormented herself by wondering which one would win his body for a night. She needed to set him free, and herself, too.

Only now there was Lilly to consider. She was in a tight spot there. During her visit to her Aunt Lucy's halfway house in St. Louis, after sneaking out on Jake, she met the girl.

She spent a few days with the bright six-year-old and felt a powerful need to give her a home. Aunt Lucy reassured Kat that the adoption process would be smooth because of her established marriage with Jake, without noticing how uneasy the conversation made Kat.

Jake was terrible at paperwork, but he didn't like when things didn't go his way. Made him more stubborn. Sheesh.

She didn't want to need him now, and he hadn't needed her in a long time. She was going to adopt the girl, and with Grandpa Eli's help, the three of them would do fine. Lilly needed a *dependable* family.

"We're not walking away from this because it's hard." Jake's tone was iron. "You being my wife is a vital part of my life, so divorce is not a consideration for me."

"Jake, I never see you, you never ask—*really ask*—how I am when you call. You clearly don't care, and I'm tired of the ride. We've become strangers since..."

Whoa. She was making the wrong argument. Maintaining the status quo was a top priority, and she needed his help to achieve it. The fights were rote with them—when they bothered.

"Listen, before I shove my foot any deeper in my mouth, since you're here and don't want a divorce, we could forget about it for a while."

The look on his face was downright scary. "What are you talking about?"

Kat mulled over the possibility of finding a peaceful resolution to this mess. She didn't need him here, just on paper.

A caseworker would make a random visit in the next three months. No one in their right mind would entrust the welfare of a child to Jake. He was a big kid himself.

She'd known him a long time and she could trust him to hunt up risk with the same energy he used to harness to ride pick-up in the arena. He'd often promised he'd never grow up. She believed him now.

"I still think we need to move on in our own directions, but we don't need to make it official." Kat was getting desperate. He wasn't budging, and she was sure he was about to demand answers. She hated that.

"I can call it off, or you can put off signing the papers until, say, next summer..." She started walking toward the house. She could distract him with a cold drink and send him on his way so she could think.

"You're unbelievable, babe." He matched her pace. "You're talking out of your head. We're not getting a divorce. Not now, not next summer, and if you don't quit bringing it up, I'm going to get mad." He kicked at a rock. "You need to be married right now, but not a month ago? Is something else going on? Is it someone else?"

He paused at the bottom of the steps, his fingers curling around the rough wood railing of her back porch. With a deep breath, he asked, "Are you... sick?"

Kat pushed past him, feeling his body heat for a moment, then took the remaining steps with a quickness. She leaned against the doorframe and turned to look at him, her heart racing.

A deep breath steadied her.

She felt gratitude swell inside her as she realized the house was empty. She wouldn't have to explain herself. That wasn't her way. She should have just let it be, but that wasn't her style, either.

"Jake, go back to the rodeo. It's where your heart is."

Jake had given up riding after an accident that landed him under his horse, leaving him with a fractured hip. He'd sworn never to get on a horse again, but rodeo consumed him more than ever.

He'd focused his rehab on being fast enough to get back in the arena, and he'd succeeded. Cowboys trusted Jake. They knew him well for his fearless antics as a clown in the circuit. But the wilder he got, the harder it was for Kat to watch. She didn't know how to tell him what she felt at first, and when she figured out, he didn't hear her.

It had been years since she left him for the last time in the little tug trailer they'd called home—until she'd gone to ask him for a divorce. Returning to the homestead she'd left behind at eighteen, she schemed a way to repurpose her old barn into a resource for her rescues.

She just told Jake she was going home for a while, then she

quit visiting. Kat wasn't even sure he noticed. Except for a few phone calls that ended in arguments and simple texts on birthdays and holidays, the years were melting away.

When they'd held each other that last night, Kat knew it was time to say goodbye. She hadn't had the courage, though. Just left the documents. Then regretted it every second since, but not for the right reasons.

Kat knew she should give it to him straight, but telling him about Lilly wouldn't do. He would provoke Kat, call the child one of her "causes." The memory of the old battle spurred her on, increasing her determination to get rid of him.

He sat down on the bottom step and fiddled with his hat, clearly determined. Scrubbing a hand through his windswept curls, he drew his cap back on. "I can't go back. I quit. Sold my truck, trailer—everything."

"You did not." She was stunned. And felt like a beast. The memory of their warm bodies tangled together in the tight bunk of Jake's trailer filled her mind. The night she left the divorce papers.

Kat shook her head, ponytail swinging. "You love your job more than... well, anything." More than her, she almost said, but she wasn't looking to fight.

"If you're telling the truth, you better go get it all back, because you can't stay here." Kat needed him to go before he discovered Lilly.

"Time to change your plans, darlin.' We're in this together, and I'm counting on you to pony up." Jake popped to his feet and casually climbed toward her. "I'll do whatever it takes to keep you."

She grabbed the screen door as a barricade. "It's too late for us, Jake. Go get your job back. My life is the ranch. Yours is the rodeo."

He covered the last two steps in a leap and slipped under her arm that was gripping the door. He kissed her. She meant to resist, but Jake's heat had always drawn her—a sensual bliss she'd once feared to live without.

Their lips met with a sizzle that sparked through her. Kat felt a soft moan of surrender escape. When he stepped back, Kat loosened her hold on his neck. Her heart felt like it would pound through her sleeveless flannel.

"I don't know, honey, I think you still like me." Jake flashed her a cocky grin. "Can I stay?"

"Toad..." Kat growled. She loosened her fists when she realized her short nails were scoring her palms. The man had skills. Staying calm was key because he'd win if she got angry.

He had to go. And keep their rocky marriage afloat.

"No, Jake, you can't stay here. There's nothing for you in this town. Don't pester me with questions. Let it go."

"Nope." He backed away from her, down the path, glancing at the flowers she'd planted last year beside the cracked sidewalk. "Sorry to break it to you, gorgeous, but I'm not going anywhere. Looks like you're stuck with me," he declared. "Honey, I'm home!"

She followed him to his bike and told herself it was to make sure he left. With a goofy grin on his face, he playfully pulled off the battered ball cap like it was a top hat and gave her a little bow.

She just shook her head, fighting a grin.

He shoved the hat in his back pocket and looked over her shoulder at her valley before slipping his shades on, the lazy river rippling and beckoning below the barn.

Nearly sixty horses stood munching around several hay rings, and there were another dozen horses in the corral beside the barn. "Despite your lack of welcome, it looks like you need a hand." He nodded at the fencing tools leaned up against the tractor. "You hiring?"

"A cowboy, not a clown. I need someone who can ride."

"You don't have to ride a horse to fence fix, darling. We can discuss my terms when I get back."

"Terms for what? We do fine here. I sure don't need you now!" Kat watched him anxiously. "Where are you going?"

He winked, and his teeth flashed in a crooked grin that mocked her. He knew she was fighting the urge to lean in and taste his lips again. She was hopeless.

He chuckled. "To find someplace to crash until you realize how much you miss me and invite me to stay with you. In the meantime, how about rustling up some grub? We'll picnic down at the river for dinner. I'll be back by dusk."

"Dream on! If you think..." Too late—he'd hopped on the bike, kick started it, and wheeled away, escaping into a cloud of dust and sunrays, oblivious to her cursing.

As he parked his bike across the street from the Inn and Out, Jake felt uneasy with the abandoned atmosphere around him. Ignoring the painful hitch in his hip, he dismounted the bike in one swift motion. The idea of being stuck in this small town had often filled him with dread, and the empty streets suggested others shared his sentiment.

There were a couple of ladies' shops open, but no cars in front. Ralph's Grocery, the vintage store that sold everything from candy to car parts, was right next to the small ad agency where he thought he remembered Lana worked. They were both open. Several of the other storefronts on the Main Street appeared vacant.

Although open, the Post office had a tired and worn-out appearance that made it seem sad and neglected. The churches had charming details such as ornate windows and intricate stonework, although they looked equally woeful. The small bank next to Tom Peabody's law office was the only new business he recognized. It looked like it was up and running, which was a good sign. He needed to grab some cash.

He was glad to see Doc Robbins still had a shingle hung outside his office. Jake always enjoyed going to see Mrs. Robbins in the small pharmacy next door. She'd trade him a bag of red licorice if he'd take the office trash out, though he hadn't always been great at holding up his end of the deal.

The small jailhouse on the square looked newly renovated, with fresh paint and shiny windows. Despite the town's challenges, Sheriff Tate's pride for his beloved town shone through, as did his vanity.

Rosati's was still ticking along, though not open at eleven on a Tuesday, but Mickey's Pizza Parlor was closed for good. Too bad. He remembered they had tasty pies, and he considered pizza a food group.

At one end of the block, there was an empty lot where Lana's apartment had been, and he wondered what the heck had happened to the entire building? It was simply gone.

Up and down Main Street, a few random open signs were out, but the lack of foot traffic made it seem deserted. He figured the parked vehicles were from shopkeepers since there were only a few.

He took a moment to appreciate the quaintness of the Inn and Out, the town's motel. His mom had texted him last week, letting him know she was staying there, and that she was expecting a visit from him soon.

She was stirring the pot, he bet. Jake needed to put a stop to her meddling, but couldn't deny that it came from a place of love. He should check in, say hello, and grab a much-needed shower... But he needed a few more minutes.

He found himself drawn toward the other end of the street to Hank's Hitchin' Post. Tossing feed for the old storekeeper was his first job. There was a realtor's packet taped to the door under a For Sale sign. Jake wondered what had happened. Hank often mentioned the notion of retirement was strange to him, so Jake doubted that was it.

His scraggly reflection in the thick layer of grime on the windows made him scowl. He wished he'd showered and shaved before going out to Kat's ranch. He rubbed the stubble along his jawline. Well. Next time.

The rodeo posters barely hanging in the window were a blast from the past, bringing back memories of hanging the signs and watching the girls in their tight jeans.

As he peered through old tape marks, he felt a sense of curiosity building within him. The barrels and bins were in the same positions as when Hank taught him to stock the shelves, when he first hired Jake to "keep him out of trouble."

As he spied the colorful silk swirling in the reflection beside him, his heart rate spiked with a surge of adrenaline.

"Mom." Turning, he opened his arms and hugged her tightly. Although her response was stiff, it was a relief that she wasn't openly hostile. "I've missed you," he said, taking in her appearance. "You look good, Mom. It's good to see you."

"Really, son? I noticed you didn't rush over to say hello to your abandoned mother."

"Don't start, Ma. Why's Hanks store closed?"

"You'd know if you bothered to check in." Tabby's touch was gentle but firm as she rubbed her hands on his shoulders. "Tell a worried mom her wild child is still breathing."

"I'm fine, Ma, look." He did a little spin for her benefit, ignoring the hitch in his hip. "Besides, when did I become wilder than Jaime?"

She crossed her arms over her ample frame. "As the two of you are twins, it's a trait you share. I see you're alive, but it remains to be seen if you're fine or not."

Jake smirked at his ma. Guilt trips were her forte and soon he'd be eating out of her hand. He wasn't about to get hooked just yet. "Hank's store?"

She nodded at the sign. "Mary passed away last winter. Since she managed the books for the store, Hank was in over his head, and he announced he was done. Lana helped him put the Hitchin' Post Farm and Feed on the market, and he hung around for a while, but when it didn't look like it was going to sell, he moved up North to be closer to the grandkids. Last I heard, he was doing fine." She nodded. "It's been for sale since. Money is tight around town, so it sits empty, and everyone drives an hour for feed. Such as life."

She aimed her beautiful blues at him, and he resisted a wince. "So, what brings you now? Have you and Kat come to a compromise?"

"Not yet, but don't worry. We're having a picnic later. Things are sure to iron out."

"Things are different here since Lana and the Wilcox boy got hitched and opened the resort. The streets are quiet, most of the tourism heads straight to the water now. But the resort is so beautiful, I can't blame them." She hesitated. "Why have you come, son? Rumor is Kat asked you for a divorce. If you're planning to stir up trouble, I recommend riding out now. Nobody wants to see that girl hurt."

"Ma, you texted me you needed a visit. How could I resist?" He gave her the grin he knew would soften her up. "I'm here, and you know I love you, but I gotta handle this myself."

Tabby sniffed. "I'll have to see it to believe it. She's a bit of a big deal around here for her work on that ranch. The horses that were getting dumped and dying out there didn't look good. Everyone worried what would happen to the Mustangs if the herds got too big. She fixed both problems, mostly by being here."

His mom licked her finger and presumably rubbed a smudge of dirt off his cheek. "If people think you don't have her interests at heart, they won't be too friendly. But who cares what we think? You just win your girl back. Your heart is your best feature. Show her your caring nature if you can find it under all that dust."

She swatted his arm. "So, let's get you checked into a room. You can stand a shower..."

"Sorry, I told Dad I was going to come out to the ranch to clean up."

"You talked to Lug?"

"Sure," Jake fibbed. If she was here, they must be in the "I'm not speaking to you" phase. That could last days or years, but he was betting they weren't speaking again.

"Hmph. Going on a picnic, huh? You got a picnic ready or you planning to share your road jerky?"

Tabby knew him so well. He was going to swing by the grocery and grab some sandwiches and chips since the bank was open. Doubtful Ralph had a card reader, and there was no way Kat was whipping up fried chicken. "I'll figure something out." He shrugged.

"The men in my family. Yeesh. You're all the same. Just waiting for someone else to work everything out for you. Well, Lug is on his own, but I rarely get to spoil you."

His mom's quick hug was a little warmer this time and Jake relaxed a hair. "Grab our old picnic basket off the shelf at the ranch, swing by here, and I'll pack it for you. Run along, now. You have a marriage to save so I can finally get a grandbaby."

Jake blushed. "It's not like that. You know Kat can't get pregnant."

"Of course not. Now run along and fetch that basket. Don't forget to shave."

He shook his head at his mom's bossiness and hightailed it out of there. He didn't plan on doing what she wanted all the time, but this time he came out ahead. At least she didn't hit him with a full to-do list. And the basket would get him points.

Chapter 2

Jake eased down the short stretch of road leading to the farm where he'd lived as a teenager. This old road made him think of Kat, and how often he'd tried to convince her to stop and make out before he took her home.

He remembered the first time he'd seen her. He was fourteen, and they'd just moved to Riverbend Falls. They'd been in town for supplies when he caught sight of her leaving the feed store with an elderly Indian fella. The moment Jake laid eyes on her, he had a feeling she was gonna be his girl.

Convincing her to take a chance on him was harder. Her passion for horses consumed her, leaving no room for anything else, especially not him. He kept at it, and he and his twin spent most of their time hanging out with Kat and Lana down at Kat's ranch. Mostly swimming in her private access, but they did chores too.

"You'll trade for any food you eat," Old Eli had insisted. He taught the four of them basic fence work, livestock feeding, and horse safety so they could do needed tasks. Jake had a place to be where he felt useful, and then he got the job at the feed store. Then he belonged.

The summer they were sixteen, Kat saw him for real, and they had been an item since. Everything went so well that summer. Lug surprised him and settled in, too. He had been in the military a long time, and he'd been rigid and surly until they came to Riverbend Falls. His folks fought less.

Before he retired early because of an injury, Lug used to fix heavy equipment and train horses for the military. They moved here and Lug built an arena to continue working horses, his passion. He started a popular multi-family rodeo once a month out at the ranch, and the four teens competed in events.

They were a tight-knit crew, and found a fair amount of adventures, despite the small town. They got banned from hanging out sometimes for being a little too rowdy, but the four of them were near inseparable. The brat pack was the nickname his mom gave them, and it fit.

He pulled his bike off the road and quieted its hum. The bike's echoes faded, and birds started tweeting. In the distance, the piercing cry of a hunting hawk echoed through the trees. It was just him and nature out here. Just him and his memories.

"Will you marry me?" It was their high school graduation, and Jake couldn't help but worry that Kat would leave him when they faced the harsh realities of adulting. He'd never wonder if she was the girl for him. He knew it in his bones. He was in love.

"We are way too young." Kat was sensible unless she was in a mood.

"I know you're the girl for me, Kat. Don't make us keep ourselves apart any more. I want the whole deal with you."

"The whole deal? Like a big, fancy wedding. With all our friends?" Kat's big brown eyes were full of a sudden wonder.

"Well, maybe not..."

"Big—Jake. And if it's the money you're worried about, we'll use mine."

"No, I'll swing whatever you need, babe. Whatever you think," he'd said. "How soon?"

"Your mom will help me plan it. I know she will. Oh, if we do this too soon, and you get itchy feet, Jake..."

"Never." He reassured her with a sexy kiss. He couldn't wait to make her his bride. It would be worth a little suffering. He'd just ask his parents to get along.

He screwed everything up, as usual. The women started getting crazy, and a few months later, he let his sister talk him into getting together for a party at the river for New Year's Eve. The weather was mild—they were eighteen and full of themselves, and needed to relax.

Bless his sister. Trouble could find Jaime wherever she was. She scored several bottles of alcohol and they proceeded to consume too much of it, cutting loose and laughing like maniacs. Next thing he knew, Sheriff Tate was shining a flashlight in their eyes, demanding to see their ID's knowing full well they were all recent graduates.

"Clearly this is your idea, Summers." Tate glared at him and his twin. "I never had any trouble out of these local girls before ya'll came here. C'mon, everyone up. You're under arrest."

"Oh, come on Sheriff," Kat wheedled. "Just give us a ride home and we won't tell that you poach deer."

"Young lady," Sheriff Tate said, blustering. "C'mon. All of you, let's go. You're in bigger trouble now, making false accusations."

Jake whispered his plan to Kat.

"We'll elope tonight, or as soon as I can get out from under my dad's thumb. Eli will never let me marry you now."

Kat agreed reluctantly, and that New Year's Eve, everything changed.

Tabby bailed the twins and Kat out, but Lana's parents were on their way to get her. Lana was scared to death, and Jake hated leaving her—they all did—but Jake had to get out of that jail and get Kat married before their folks all decided he was unfit.

Jake and Jaime snuck out shortly after their parents finished lecturing them and met Kat. They drove all night, and he married Kat the next morning, with Jaime as the only witness to their Vegas wedding.

The timing was awful. They heard a few hours later that Lana's parents were killed in a car accident the night before. Thankfully, Lana survived, and deserting her now felt terrible, but the twins decided there was no way they were going back to face their folks, and Kat stuck with him.

That night, they agreed to chase their futures, and they were all scared.

"Come with us, Jaime," Kat begged.

Jaime gave Kat a look. "Don't be some stupid bunny, Kat. Girls of our caliber don't belong sleeping in parking lots." Jaime had given him a disdainful look. "And you, brother, wouldn't be asking her to do this if you had a heart. She doesn't like to see animals hurt, c'mon."

He flinched. "It's not about that and you know it."

Jaime shook her head. "Nope, I'm out. I'm enrolling in a Job Corps and ya'll are looking at a future culinary genius." Jaime grinned when Jake almost had a laughing fit. "Whatever. You know you'll eat anything I'll make." She laughed good-naturedly and poked Kat in the arm. "I'll give you some lessons once I get good."

Jake could tell Kat was miserable. Kat didn't want Jaime to leave, and neither did he. He didn't think Kat would be as enthusiastic as he was about the new travel trailer he just bought them, and he'd been hoping Jaime would soften her up, make it sound fun. His twin was ditching him, but he got the girl. Kat was his world... He'd take it as a win, despite the damage his win cost them all.

Saying goodbye felt like ripping off a band-aid, and they all knew it was going to hurt for a while.

He shook his head, sending the memory away. He knew both Kat and Jaime stayed in constant contact with Lana, but he'd never really looked back.

Jake wished he knew what Kat's deal was now. He thought they had a decent marriage. Most folks didn't seem to make it very long anymore, and he was determined not to be a quitter.

How did he not see this coming? He thought she came here to play with her horses. True, she never came to watch him anymore, but he figured it was because he didn't ride. She'd always been all about the horses.

He hadn't realized it had been so long since they'd seen each other until Kat came to see him—*to divorce him*—and he knew how much he missed her. She always saw the best in every situation, every person. He needed her light, but he wished he didn't have to come here to see it.

This place made him feel like a failure. He wouldn't stand still for that. Jake not only made decent money, but he was a hit with the crowds.

He only seemed to fail in the expectations of folks in this town, who didn't matter, and his woman, who did. With Kat, he had to give her head—she was going to do what she wanted, anyway.

What she wanted was still the dad gum horses.

As a kid, she and a group of others crusaded for federal protection for the three wild horse herds ranging on the land above her family's ranch and won it for them. Now she rescued tame horses people dumped off outside the preserve that couldn't survive in the wild. The cost of feed alone had to be gouging her.

Now if there was an animal on this earth he didn't trust, it was a horse. Even years later, he could still recall the feeling of helplessness he experienced while suspended on his back in the hospital. It sucks to be trampled by your own horse.

He worked hard to be one of the best clowns in the circuit so he could save other cowboys from the feeling. Not as many as when he used to ride pick-up, but he did what he could without a horse.

He knew that Kat's passion for saving the world would eventually take her away from him, but he wished it wasn't because of her responsibility to protect the horses. Here. His folks always make him hyper-aware of his own imperfections. He fired up his bike and finished the short drive to his old man's ranch.

Time to face Lug.

Kat sat at her kitchen table idly spinning a glass of her lavender-mint tea, ice melted hours ago. A heavy sigh escaped her lips, and she couldn't shake off the feeling of disappointment.

Lilly came home from school acting withdrawn, and though she and Eli were upstairs playing a game, there were none of the cheerful noises and hoots of laughter coming down the stairs that Kat had learned to look forward to.

She worried Lilly would fall into the old patterns of fighting at school that Aunt Lucy had warned her about. She needed to start making friends soon.

Work had been a pain today. She'd had to jump the tractor to feed round bales, so she'd need a new battery before winter. Kat needed the fencing on the back forty acres so she could range another dozen horses on the back side in the spring. She was getting crowded, but adoptions had fallen way off.

As if the strain of rising grain and fuel costs weren't enough, the sight of another abandoned horse that morning only added to her worries about how to feed everyone. The appaloosa was underfed and homely, but thankfully not injured. She loved it already.

It infuriated her that people thought dumping a tame animal in the wild was going to help feed them. The horse seemed relieved to see the grain bucket Kat carried and had gladly followed her away from the river near where the wild herds grazed into her pasture.

Then there was Jake. If she hadn't asked him for a divorce, he might never have realized things were not okay. She'd bet the ranch on it. Now she was in a bind.

She rested her chin on her fist, wishing. The late afternoon sunrays were streaming through the open kitchen window, past her window boxes, filling her nose with scents of lavender, mint, and freshly mown hay. She tried to rouse herself, knowing she needed to pull something together for dinner.

She didn't know if Jake would come back or not. Most likely he was long gone—he probably couldn't handle one afternoon in town. She frowned. Hopefully, he wasn't preparing to complicate her life. She never knew what to expect from him, though.

She'd been married for twelve years—since she was eighteen. Jake's haphazard methods weren't unexpected, it was just something she wasn't ready for right now. And he was a stickler for doing things right.

If she couldn't get rid of Jake before he discovered she was using their sham of a marriage to get custody of Lilly, he might expose her as a fraud.

The noise of his bike rumbling up the driveway made her groan in frustration. She glanced at her dirty jeans and boots, feeling a pang of regret for not cleaning up.

She'd been a hot mess all afternoon, sorting and banning jumbled memories. Kat was in no condition to argue—and she certainly hadn't prepared him a picnic. She'd just convince him to leave, and quick.

She grabbed her jacket from the hook in the mudroom and walked out the back door. Kat wouldn't give him a chance to get into the house. Eli and Lilly were still upstairs, and she hoped they'd stay occupied while she got rid of Jake.

"I told you I'm not going out with you."

"Yet here I am." Jake was just rounding the corner to the back porch, and he was holding suspiciously familiar flowers.

She came down the wide steps, and he handed her the bright bunch. His mom's basket was slung over his arm, triggering wonderful memories of picnics and swimming trips. Tabby would often pack the four teens into her beat-up station wagon and take them on an adventure to some new river or lake in the Ozarks she'd discovered. Whenever Tabby rallied them on a summer afternoon, they knew they were in for a treat with her overflowing basket of goodies.

Kat had loved the twin's mom like her own and when she was planning the wedding, Tabby had been like she imagined her own Mom would have been. When she eloped with Jake, all the dynamics changed and the twins' folks separated.

She hadn't seen the basket in a long time. He surprised her with a smooth kiss that didn't fail to curl her toes.

"You might want to put these in water. I just picked them."

"Did you pick my flowers?" Kat glared at him. "You're unbelievable." She inhaled the flowers, trying to ignore the feelings stirring in her. The shadows under his eyes just added to his rugged appeal, and she found herself drawn to him. Against her better judgement, she played nice.

"We can take a short walk and you can tell me what you have in that basket. I haven't seen that since..." *Since his folks split up the first time, another banned topic.* She gave him a careful look. "Have you seen your parents?"

"Yes, and no." Jake lifted his cap and ran his fingers through his curls before turning to the path that would lead to their favorite big, flat, make out rock by the river's edge.

Jake was aggravated and Kat quick stepped to catch up.

"Yes, and no?"

"Yes, I saw them both. No, I won't tell ya what's in the basket. We gotta hash out the divorce you wanted and now don't. I suspect this is one of your causes—certainly more likely than you changing your mind about something. You're the most stubborn... anyway, what are you hiding?"

"Nothing." She stopped him, her hand on his arm to halt his progress. "Nothing you'd be interested in. I've barely seen you in two years, except when I brought the papers. My lawyer says..."

"Does Tom know we had hot monkey sex less than two months ago and neither of us left the bed feeling less than satisfied?"

He was looking at her with that stubborn glint in his eyes, and it made her nervous. As usual, she was making a mess. "Look, Jake, say I welcomed you with open arms? What do you want?"

"I don't want to lose you, that's for sure. But—"

"You would *want* to settle here in Riverbend Falls and—"

Behind them, a screen door slammed and Lilly came running down the hill, followed by an interested looking Grandpa Eli.

"Mom, Grandpa Eli said we should get some air, too. Can we come with you?"

Lilly gave Jake a shy glance and Kat worried. The child was so fragile. Kat wished Lilly had an easier start, but if she had anything to say about it, things would be better for her now. If she could keep from screwing this up.

"Sure, hon. Let's tie your shoe while Grandpa catches up, okay? Then you can look for shells on the bank. This fella and I have things to talk about."

"All right, but I can do it." Lilly tied her sneaker, then gave Jake a look that seemed to size him up and dismiss him. Then she waited for Eli to catch up.

Jake crouched down, bringing Lilly's focus back to him. "Hey, scout... This is amazing, meeting you. Me and your mom were sorting out some big stuff."

He shot Kat a look that was both befuddled and wounded.

"I think we've just about got things hammered out for a piece. I won't keep her from ya. Ya'll have a good time and be sure not to let a crawdad get your nose." He tweaked her nose, and she giggled.

Kat's heart was pounding. Every passing second felt like a ticking time bomb, ready to explode any moment.

"Jakob." Eli strode up, clutching his walking staff in his gnarled hand. He didn't need it to shore up his spry frame, but he usually carried it. Jake received a passing glance, as if he came often.

He used to be intimidated by her grandfather, but Lilly's words had surprised Jake—he was trying to put things together, and she could tell from the look in his eye he hadn't figured it out yet. Kat should have explained sooner, and Grandpa Eli should have kept Lilly inside!

"Eli." Jake dipped his head.

Eli seemed proud of himself as he told Kat, "Lilly needed some air. We'll be close if you need us." With a sparkle in his eye, he briefly eyed the Summers picnic basket before being distracted by Lilly as she grabbed his hand and pulled him down to the water's edge.

Kat looked after them, a yearning for family thick in her throat with Jake standing so near. She needed to get her thoughts together. He wouldn't be pushed into the dad role by her.

The idea of getting custody of Lilly as a single parent was intimidating, but she was up for the challenge. She had to respect Jake's choice of not wanting to be a parent. The moment had finally arrived, and she knew he would agree to the divorce.

As soon as she saw his expression, Kat knew she didn't need to explain herself. She could see it in his eyes. As Jake backed away, his eyes darted around, searching for a means of escape.

"Mom?" He was staggered, like he'd taken a hoof to the gut. That Kat had become a parent without him noticing was not possible, unless... they had been distant with each other since— *a very long time.*

Surely she hadn't been hiding this child. He looked at the little girl again. She was small, had to be about five or six, though. She looked like Kat with that silky dark hair, a dark complexion, and deep eyes. There wasn't a trace of Summers in the girl. He looked at Kat, knowing the betrayal he felt was on his face.

He set the basket down on the ground. Kat was watching the old man and the skipping girl with an odd expression, and it was too much. "Mom's fried chicken. Enjoy it with your family."

He turned and walked away. Climbing on his bike, he steered away from the hurt. He stopped at the park across from where Lana's apartment used to be. It wasn't the only weird thing going on here. None of it made sense, and Jake was sure he was missing something.

He would have known if she'd had a child.

It had been a lot of years since they properly lived together, but his job was all travel. She hadn't minded until she'd wanted to have a baby. That had been the most wretched experiment of their lives. He still didn't think Kat had moved past it.

So where does she get a little kid who calls her Mom? And why does she still "need" to be married for now?

Jake wheeled his bike around toward his dad's place. It sounded to him like Kat had found another cause, and unless he was misreading her, she was trying to pull a fast one.

He wasn't leaving without winning his wife back.

The chill air cleared his mind as he rode the curvy back road to his dad's place to crash for the night, despite knowing he was riding into a hornet's nest of family obligations. Whatever the heck Kat was up to, he knew she'd bargain for it, and then he'd get what he wanted—her.

Jake muffled his bike as he approached the familiar longhorn skull hanging over the fence railing for the second time that day. When he'd come earlier, his dad had been passed out on the couch, TV blaring old Gunsmoke reruns and a six-pack of crumpled beer cans on the coffee table next to him.

It was obvious Tabby wasn't staying in the old farmhouse.

He'd left his dad on the couch without waking him. Idly, he wondered if his dad would be in the same position now.

The porch light was off, but as soon as his feet hit the dirt, Lug spoke up from the front porch swing. Jake could see him in the shadows, swaying gently.

"I wondered if you'd be back, boy. Why are you here? No work for a clown around these parts."

Jake ground his teeth and grabbed his trusty cap from his back pocket.

Ready for anything now, right?

He longed for a simple, "I've missed you, son."

Negative. Affection was something his father didn't cotton to. Andrew "Lug" Summers turned to rodeo after his military service, but his drive to make his children excel in the sport caused their family to fall apart.

When Jake lost his chance at the big time, and almost died, he came back better than ever, just reinvented. Lug disapproved of the clown job, even making the effort to come and ridicule him in person.

"If you're not on a horse, you're not doing your best. If you're not doing your best, you're wasting your time. In the military, boy, you just get back on and do your job."

Ole Lug sure knew how to cut him. He wouldn't be riding.

Would he have stuck so hard if it hadn't ticked his dad off?

Probably. He craved attention. Being noticed was being noticed. "I came back for Kat. On my way through town from her place, I noticed Hanks was—"

"If you've seen your wife, what are you doing here? Some reason you aren't sleeping with her?" His dad stood up. "Don't make the same mistakes I did, boy. You got to get your woman figured out before it's too late and you're too old to change. I thought maybe…"

He walked into the house and, almost as an afterthought, he called out through the screen door. "Feel free to bunk in your old room, son, but if I were you, I'd be down at the river convincing your gal to take you back."

The sound of Lug's voice, now sober and gruff, made him

rethink his impulse to argue. He bit his cheek and followed him inside. Exhaustion weighed heavily on him, but he knew he had to come up with a strategy soon.

Jake would need a job. His ma was right about that.

He'd grown weary of the rumors that he was only with Kat for her money, and he wished people would mind their own business. Jake had a tidy amount of savings, but if he wasn't working at something in this town, they'd still call him shiftless.

As he stepped over Rusty, the old redbone hound lying on the porch, he couldn't shake the plan about Hanks from his head, and went inside to grill his dad. He was hoping it would help him forget the spicy hot taste of Kat, so he could sleep.

Chapter 3

The moment Kat opened her eyes, she felt the sharp pain of a headache that had been lurking all night. She beelined to the bathroom, grabbed a few ibuprofens and winced at the sight of her reflection in the smoke edged glass medicine cabinet.

Ugh. She felt lousy and thought she might be getting sick. Just great. She dressed in a t-shirt and jeans after taking a long shower and headed downstairs to make toast.

She tested her blood sugar. It was a little low, so she called Doc Robbin's office to schedule a quick checkup, but he was on vacation until Monday. It was likely just stress, but with her history, she booked the appointment anyway.

Eli liked to jaw around at the sale barn on Wednesdays, always looking for suitable homes for the horses, so he drove Lilly to school and dropped her on his way. Kat grinned at the way the two of them were bonding. Having Lilly around had changed Kat's relationship with Eli, too.

When she first came home, Jake's mom had tracked them down in San Antonio and told them that Eli had suffered a minor stroke. Growing up, Grandpa Eli had been her protector, and now it was her turn to take care of him.

She begged Jake to come with her and stay at the ranch, but he was too stubborn. He was firm in his decision to pay for both of them, brushing off her offer to cover his costs, let alone her own. He had to make his mark first, earn his way. She was going to help Eli with work on the ranch, and she left Jake and his love for the thrill of danger behind.

She used to love watching his fearless riding, but the accident made her too fearful to watch. When she sat with him at the hospital, she saw the resignation in his eyes and believed he was done with the circuit. Despite her hopes that he would slow down, his wild streak returned with a vengeance. Only he quit riding and started courting death on foot in rags and a Kevlar vest.

Talking about her feelings always ended up in a fight. She'd finally stopped showing up, and the only contact they had was sporadic phone calls or texts to keep in touch.

As soon as she got home, she felt lost and needed something to distract her from constant memories of Jake. She discovered a new sense of purpose when she saw how many domestic horses were not mingling with the wild ones. She contacted her old coalition and started the paperwork to allow her to home the overflow.

Her parents died within a few years of adopting her, but they'd left Eli to raise her and willed her the beautiful land that was situated next to the land where the wild horse herds roamed. Her mother had loved the horses so.

One of her biggest challenges now was keeping enough of it fenced for grazing year-round. With the cost of gas and the added expense of driving 50 miles for licks and grain, she felt the financial strain.

She had created a website as a platform to find adoptive homes for the horses, aiming to defray the costs of their upkeep. Kat only asked for a small adoption fee to cover the horse's costs and make sure the new owners were serious. She poured all her sales money into her mission and used her own money to do massive upgrades in her barns and stable.

Once Eli regained his health, he'd become stubborn and obtuse. He'd said her fussing around him was "suffocating," and moved to the stable. It didn't bother her since her outbuildings were better than the house and the stable room was a little apartment meant for a cowboy, but she'd grown used to having him around. Kat and the old man worked the ranch together, but they had their own ways of doing things, so it wasn't always harmonious.

Since Lilly turned the old man into a teddy bear, Eli had been visiting the house more often. The old place was becoming a home. She was still only a temporary guardian until the adoption was formalized, but Kat's emotions had swelled when the little girl shyly asked if she could call her Mom because she'd always wanted one.

A crease formed on Kat's forehead as she contemplated that. Did Lilly want a dad, too? I mean, of course she did, but...

Time to get her act together, stop wool gathering. Jake would be long gone by now. She should count that as a mark of success. Today was going to be a big day, and as she buttered her toast, she hoped her cowboy would show up.

Park was the lone cowboy for hire in the area, leaving her with limited options. He was unreliable at best, and she didn't like his dad, but she was more worried about the odd vibes Park gave her, like he was picturing her naked or something.

She had to have someone to ride fences, though. With winter closing in, she was going to be in a bind for space soon, so she'd take what she could get.

She brewed a fresh pot of coffee and gathered up her work list for the day and a few carrots and an apple. She set to mucking stalls and quickly finished, leading the horses back into the barn two by two. Kat only stabled her own dozen horses, but she'd built lean-to's in the field for the rescue horses.

She stroked the nose of her favorite big guy, Dream, and shared an apple with the buckskin. He had been lounging in the corral, waiting for her, hoping she'd take him for a ride.

No time, yet again.

The ranch hand, his big diesel truck belching black smoke, finally pulled up. She gave him a quick tour of the barn, introducing her horses to him, then asked him to set out her last lick bucket down by the water before heading out to inspect the fence that Eli suspected had been tampered with.

Some people weren't happy about the wild horses, claiming

the land they roamed on was prime land, land they wanted to use. She fenced right up to the federal land, and there were a lot of fishermen and boaters who wished she'd go back to ignoring her property lines.

As if it wasn't enough to stretch a new fence, sometimes she had to repair malicious damage, as well as the regular worn sections. She let their meanness wash off her, though. The horses were her true love. If they were lucky, they might have an extra set of hands to help them through the winter. If she could put up with Park's ogling.

She ducked into the barn to check on Potato Chip. He'd wanted to stay in his stall this morning, and she thought he looked a little worn out now. Old Chip was blind, and she suspected he only had partial hearing, but a sweeter horse she'd never met. Kat took him in after they found him and made him family. She fed him some grain and crooned wistfully in his ear before moving on, promising herself she'd check on him again this evening.

She hadn't named the newest horse, bless his homely heart. He hadn't started socializing with the other horses, and she was giving him time. She gave him a little extra grain and vowed to toughen up enough for them both.

Her attention was drawn to the ATV parked just outside the barn. She shouldn't have invested in it, but she'd worried if any one came out to ride and got hurt, she might not coax them back on their horse if they were on the trails, so she'd bought it. Kat had one rotten experience and hoped never to ride the unfeeling beast again.

She could see the usefulness of tractors, though.

Her favorite was an old Jubilee that had a million miles on it. Kat could fix it herself, and cut, raked, and baled squares twice a year with it. Still, she trusted horses over mechanical beasts that would quit on ya in the middle of nowhere, maybe in the middle of a job!

Now a horse, there's a dependable creature.

It seemed most people had forgotten it, though. Despite their best efforts, the shelter struggled to find homes for their animals over the summer months.

The resort was a stunning addition to Riverbend Falls, down by the river and given the name Falls Mill by her best friend and her new man, but Kat hadn't figured out how to make it benefit her horses. Or her town. What tourism was passing through wasn't stopping in town much beyond buying ice at the filling station.

It didn't help that if you had to make the Crestview run for feed, then you probably got all your goods there and the shopkeepers who were open here, well, they miss out, anyway. She still made a dedicated effort to get her groceries from Ralph, though, and she knew several others did, too.

It was just a pain. She hadn't had to leave the Falls much since she came home until the feed store closed. She used to get everything she needed with one swing around Main Street.

But it was a chore that had to be done.

With classic bad timing, as she was about to leave, Jake came cruising up her road. His bike seemed quieter, or at least the horses seemed to tolerate the roar of the machine better today. Jake was glaring at Park's pickup in her driveway, and she wondered if she was going to have to back him down. Hopefully, there wouldn't be yelling. Just her luck.

She'd been debating whether to ask him for help with Lilly if he came back, but she still hoped he'd disappear instead. Then she'd have more time to be sure of her feelings.

She wanted to be done with him. Didn't she? She yearned for the comfort of crawling into bed at night without the weight of his absence on her mind.

If only she hadn't asked for a divorce, he would be facing down some ticked off bull to the wild cheers and adoration of hundreds of his fans. Jake Summers had become such a heartthrob among women of all ages that they had started a fan club for him.

He wouldn't likely gather praise here. What was he doing? He didn't want this. He'd never looked back at these hills.

"So, who's rig?"

The underlying accusation in his tone ticked her off. Really?

He was judging her? Mr. oh yeah, I didn't notice it's been two years since I saw your face—how are you? Well. She was desperate. Ragland called, and she hired him.

"Jealous, Jake? Save it. We're past that. What do you want? I told you yesterday, I'd prefer you just go back to what you were doing. It seems I was wrong. I'd rather miss you than divorce you, but I can't miss you if you won't go away."

Kat's voice was sharp and cutting, and she couldn't help but wish she could soften it. This was not the way to get him to help, but he always brought the richest sarcasm out of her.

Another of his gifts, she thought as she checked out his tanned and toned body. His charm and inconsistency were both irresistible and infuriating.

"So, it is a boyfriend?" He scowled, looking like he was on the verge of charging off and beating up the man.

"No, it's Park Ragland, the only cowboy left in the area not working somewhere. You might remember him from school? He's familiarizing himself with the territory, and I have errands to run, so I'm not free to visit with you. Not that it's any of your business."

His business or not, she prayed he'd leave. The wagging tongues in Riverbend Falls had more than enough practice discussing the affairs of Jake and Kat.

She'd rebuilt her reputation the last few years, but small towns... one big dramatic lovers' quarrel was all it would take to make them the focus of gossip again, and she knew neither of them wanted that.

"So, what's it going to take to get you to go?" she asked.

He grinned at her lazily and hitched his thumb in his belt loop. When he started kicking up a dust with his scuffed leather boot, she figured she was going to have to pry it out of him.

"We need to talk," he said. "So, sure. I'll go."

He had something on his mind, something big. She could always tell when he went into his "I can wheedle my way out of trouble" stance, which reminded her of a mischievous little boy. It was unconscious, and it so worked. Hmph.

But she was relieved.

"Good. I need to drive over to the feed store in Crestview before the bus brings Lilly home." The mirrored look of relief on his face puzzled her.

"Perfect. Solves all our problems. I wanted to talk to you about the feed store. I'll ride with you and check out the competition." He flashed his megawatt smile, and she took the bait.

"Ride with? No. Competition?" Kat knew she had no chance of getting her way, and now she was curious. What was he up to?

"Yep." He gave a half bow, his face beaming with warmth. "You're looking at the new owner of Hank's Hitchin' Post."

"You... you what? I mean, I heard you, but... you just bought a business? Why would you—the feed store? I'm babbling." She leaned against her pickup, staring at him in disbelief. "Jake, since the accident, well, let's just say, with you rodeo started as a fever and turned into a disease. I don't see you leaving the limelight. Do you even know how to run a business?"

She shook her ponytail in disbelief as he loped around and opened the passenger door.

"Exactly why I need your help, Kat. Let's plan a grand celebration for the re-opening and donate the proceeds to a good cause. It's something you can get into." With a crafty look in his eyes, he got into the truck. He said, "You drive. I'll do the talking."

She knew she was in for a fascinating ride.

With something between an exasperated sigh and a lusty groan, she wondered if the lengthy drive would leave her sanity intact. It was as if Jake had a magnetic energy that attracted chaos and excitement.

Try as she might, she couldn't resist getting tangled up in his schemes. With the scorching kiss yesterday close to her mind, she got behind the wheel, remembering summer nights spent necking in this truck—the same truck she'd been driving in the hayfields since she was nine.

Her cheeks flushed, and she was determined to talk about something other than their relationship, or lack thereof. If it had to be Jake's nutty new plan, she was in.

He had other ideas. He propped his hands behind his head and stretched his feet out, his 6-foot frame filling the Ford like water in a pond. "So, who's Lilly's father? Clearly, I'm not. Are you her Mom?"

As she turned onto Highway QQ from Old River Road, she raised an eyebrow at him inquisitively. His expression confirmed what she thought she heard. His lack of trust hurt her feelings, but they hadn't been on the same page for a while. Conceivably, Kat could have hidden a child from him.

And telling him about Lilly hadn't been her plan. Still, it rankled.

"Really, Jake? Do you think I've been hiding a child from you for six years?" Checking the rearview, she was relieved there was no traffic and took a longer glance at him.

He was staring her down, waiting for an answer.

"Look, Lilly's not my daughter either. Yet. I stopped to see Aunt Lucy on my way home after I... visited you. Lilly was one of her fosters. Her mother died when she was born and she's been in the system since. She's had a tough time with homes and she gets despondent sometimes, which is why no one's adopted her yet. Just like me."

Kat looked over at Jake to see how he was taking all this in, but he was just listening, the muscle in his jaw jumping up and down the only sign of his aggravation.

"She also started fighting in her last school. They think perhaps she may have suffered some mental abuse in her first home, but she claims to have no memories of the events." Kat's stomach churned as she told more of Lilly's story, feeling a compounding worry about how he was accepting the news of their adoption.

"She's been through a lot for a little girl," Kat said. "She had some tough times before she landed at Aunt Lucy's and she gets withdrawn sometimes. Six times in her brief life, she's been denied a home to call her own. I applied to adopt her."

Since they were married, she included Jake's name on the application. She hoped he wouldn't be uncompromising, but she'd never planned for him to show up at all! Things were spiraling out of control, and Kat felt guilty for her good intentions again.

His voice had an edge to it and she had a feeling they were on the ridge of one of their glorious fights. "You don't want to stay married because you still love me, but because you believe it will help you with your latest cause," he said. "So, you're using me and the girl?"

She flinched, feeling a sharp pain in her heart. He let out a deep growl of frustration as he shifted his hostile gaze away from her. She wanted to comfort him, but the divide between them had grown too great.

A deep sigh escaped Kat. The storm brewing in the East matched her dark mood with its deep gray thunderheads. She had a massive headache, likely from dealing with her man-child husband.

"She's not a cause, Jake, she's a child who needs—"

"Exactly, Kat. Why do I always have to struggle to get your attention, while others seem to have it so easily? You share your heart with strangers, but the man who loves you receives divorce papers. What did we miss?" he asked, frustration clear in his tone.

"You never need me, Jake!" She pounded her palm against the steering wheel, trying to release her anger. "Forget it. I'm not having this argument with you again. You're right. I'm never there for you. I think you should want a divorce. You're right, though. I'm afraid I sort of need you now. 'Happily married' were the words Aunt Lucy used when she assured me I wouldn't have trouble getting full custody."

She was getting ticked off, thinking about how happily married she was, but she tried to keep it together. If she wasn't so emotional, they might talk. Kat tried to moderate her tone.

"I'm expecting an unplanned visit from a caseworker sometime between now and Thanksgiving, a visit that will decide whether Lilly is permanent or temporary. When I asked for the divorce, I did not know about Lilly, Jake. I didn't mean to hurt you. We've outgrown each other, and staying together would only prolong the inevitable, but I just need you to wait until I can get Lilly…"

The look of disdain he gave her caused a searing pain in her icy heart. She had to be honest though. Well—at least now that she was busted.

"Are you seriously going to label me as a deadbeat dad without even talking to me, when I believe being a parent is an immense responsibility?"

She pulled off the road before heading to the feed store. This wasn't a conversation she wanted to continue where anyone could overhear.

"Yes. You make it sound much more terrible than it is—was—whatever, but it's still what I want." She leaned back against the seat and closed her eyes briefly. "I know you don't want to have children, Jake. Never wanted them, but I want Lilly. I want to make a home for her."

"Come on, Kat, stop being selfish. It's been a long time since we discussed starting a family—"

"Because it's an unequivocal 'no' with you—same as riding. We haven't been able to have a civil conversation about anything with substance since… We haven't been there for each other in a long time." She reached over to him. "I've made peace with the fact we've lost our way. That hasn't changed for me, but I need your help. Will you help me get custody of Lilly?"

He jerked back from her outstretched hand. "I don't want to lose you, so I don't think we should risk you getting pregnant. But we never talked about adoption. Being used and made a fool of doesn't sit well with me, Karita. I can tell the kid means a lot to you. Let me wrap my head around it." He took a deep breath. "We should float this weekend. Like back in the day, but with Lilly, so I can get to know her."

As he nodded at the dash of her truck, she couldn't help but wonder if he was judging her. His choice to help her adopt Lilly would alter everything. She herself was still getting used to the change, and the fear of losing it all loomed over her.

Cussing was still her worst habit, and she'd been making a dedicated effort not to swear anymore. Jake made her temper hard to hold. He didn't take no for an answer.

"We could load up sodas and sandwiches and make a date of it." He looked at her hard, not quite a peace offering.

She shook her head in frustration. "I don't want to date you, Jake. We need to do what's best for Lilly and I think you being around will only confuse her. I don't know right now where you fit into the life I'm building... What if Lilly gets attached to you but you get bored with the scenery and jet?"

She almost let it slip that she'd be okay with him being around. How had they grown so far apart when they knew each other so well—fit so perfectly?

"That was always your problem, Kat. You want to save the entire world, but you won't take a chance on us. We need fun— it's the only way we can stay young. I won't let you drive me off just so you can wrap yourself so tight you turn into an old lady."

"You made me into an anxious old lady, fearing for your safety against a raging bull!" She was seething with anger, her breathing ragged as she tried to calm herself down. "I couldn't take worrying about you anymore. I'm ready to adult—it doesn't scare me anymore. Let's be real. You're never gonna get there."

He covered the space between them on the seat, his lips passionately claiming hers. The kiss was so intense she reveled in him until he pulled away for air.

"You can lie to yourself, Kat, but you never could hide your emotions. You want me."

"What a jerk. I've always wanted you. Sex isn't the problem." He leaned back, giving her plenty of space. She rubbed her hands over her face tiredly, trying to tell herself her lips weren't tingling with need. "Look, I don't want to rehash this. Please, what can I do to convince you we are not right for each other? I just need you to go back on the road..."

"Nope. I bought the store and I'm staying in Riverbend Falls. Forever. With you, I s'pose." He held his hand up, stalling her protest. "I'll be planning to stay at your ranch, and after we discuss things with Lilly, you and I can discuss our sleeping arrangements. What?" He turned his palm up in an innocent gesture. "At least I'm not asking you for break-up sex."

He glanced at the approaching clouds.

"Looks like a nasty storm heading our way." He turned and looked her up and down speculatively, a suggestive leer in his blue eyes. "Listen. I think it's time for some deal making. You need help with Lilly and I need help with the feed store. We're gonna play house until Thanksgiving and you're gonna work your fanny off to help me be open by October's end. Then we'll go from there."

"How can you be serious about the store? You know nothing about running a business. The only skills you have are—"

"Thanks for believing in me." He huffed. "I know I'm a clown, but while you were busy saving the world, I've become successful. I've had five guys working for me at every rodeo gig I do. I deal with crazy fans and bulls that are way wilder than any of these old ranchers who might get all riled up over things I did when I was younger. Don't worry, I got this. And I'll have company, dear wife. You can give me pointers."

He paused, and the anger she knew was simmering in him was challenging his reserve. Unfortunately, she was mad enough to spit nails.

"I told you I wanted you back," he continued. "Now I'm not so sure. Honestly, adopting a kid using an absent father is sneaky, even for you. You made this mess for us, though, and we'll have to see how it plays out. I'll work on a plan. In the meantime, we better get a move on so we can get your feed and get home to unload before the storm breaks."

Her eyes flicked toward him, nervousness bubbling up at the gruffness in his voice. There was something in his tone that made Kat want to retreat, something that was far from pleasant.

With the truck in gear, the sound of the engine filled the cab and muffled the howling wind outside. They didn't say a sociable word to each other for the rest of the trip.

Chapter 4

Dinner was quite an event. Lilly was fine with Jake staying, but Eli wasn't having it. Throughout the meal, he grumbled about the sanctity of marriage under his breath while giving Jake and Kat dirty looks. He didn't buy Jake's story about being home for good.

It was unbelievable to Kat. For years, she had hoped that Jake would return home and decide to live and work in the Falls. It amazed her he contacted the realtor himself, and made an offer on the property, but ultimately, she questioned his follow through.

Even with the resort becoming a sensational destination place, the area would still bore Jake. He needed the spotlight.

"Can I have another piece of cherry pie?" Jake asked, and flashed Lilly a grin. "You want to split a piece with me, kiddo?"

"Sure. Mom makes the best pie."

Her loyalty was much sweeter than the naturally sweetened pie, Kat thought. Lilly held out a licked clean dessert plate for her half of the slice and mumbled a thanks as she spooned up another bite.

Kat stood up and took the last piece over to Eli, trying to butter him up. "I sure love having such a hungry bunch. Makes my cooking seem a lot more practical." She rested her hand on the old man's shoulder to settle him, but she was pretty sure Jake was trying to keep Eli ruffled up.

Jake and Eli hadn't seen eye to eye after she eloped with Jake. When Kat came back alone, Eli was more irritated than ever. No way to win with him.

She just had to get things smoothed out for all their sakes. Jake's idea was a good one and if he was serious about making a try, she would, too.

She had nothing to lose except Lilly—the marriage she had already given up on. Jake spoke, his lyrical voice pulling at Kat's romantic streak, but his words were all wrong.

"So, Lilly, since we're going to be a family, if you want to call me dad, it's okay with me. Me and your mom are going to be just a regular family now, and with your Grandpa Eli's help," he gave Eli a pointed look that had the old man stiffening under her hand, "we'll be such a great family, that your caseworker won't have any choice but to let you stay here and be our daughter."

The glimmer in Lilly's eyes was unmistakable, and Kat's heart was racing in response. She became conscious of her tight grip on Eli's shoulder and quickly released him with a gentle pat before moving to clear the table. Jake was promising too much, way too fast.

He was clueless about the responsibilities of being that little girl's father. Her own eye had a tear in it. So many times, Jake made golden promises. He just couldn't keep them. He wasn't lying—right now he believed he could do it. She wanted to believe.

Kat grabbed plates from the table and took them to the kitchen, stacking them in the sink. She leaned over the new countertop and stared at the glossy patterns inlaid in the marble. She took a few deep breaths. In two weeks, when the shiny wears off and he realizes he has somewhere he needs to be...

"I know what you're thinking, Kat. It was all over your face out there."

His voice startled her. She hadn't heard the door swing open behind her. "Jake..."

He gripped her shoulders, turning her to face him. "It's gonna be different this time, babe. I want you and if you want to play house, that's what I want. I know you think I'll get bored or distracted, and I can promise you I won't always be as straight and narrow as you wish I was, but I'll try for you. This store thing, us adopting Lilly... we always win against the world when we work together, Kat. It's a relief we can have a family without going through... you know. Let's adopt as many kids as you want, as long as we don't take that risk again. I like kids, you know that."

She rested her head against his chest. "I'm afraid it's too good to be true, but if you're sure, yeah, let's give it a go."

Kat felt her eyes leaking, and she wiped them with the back of her hand and pulled back. She was not a crier. She wished she knew why she felt so freaking emotional lately. There was so much drama twisting in the wind, and it was chaos to her orderly and simple soul.

"So, let's go on a canoe float Saturday. We'll just relax and get current. Say yes."

"Okay." She relented, figuring what was the worst that could happen? They'd get ready to go and Jake would bail at the last minute because something came up? So what? She'd learned not to wait for Jake. If he didn't come, she'd just canoe with Lilly alone.

Saturday morning, that's exactly what happened. When Jake didn't show up at the landing, the two girls set off without him. They'd been floating for almost an hour, and Kat was trying to keep Lilly entertained, but the girl was having none of it. Kat was aggravated at Jake for giving Lilly false hopes. She was used to it, but Lilly wasn't.

"Look!" Lilly twisted around, looking behind her, and Kat turned to see Jake energetically paddling a kayak toward them. She slid her paddle into the water, braking to wait for him.

"I knew he'd come," Lilly whispered under her breath, and Kat was sorry. If she was going to have a chance of making them a family, she was going to have to give Jake a little more credit. When he pulled up alongside them, he reached over and tweaked Lilly's nose, then gave Kat a special smile.

"Well, I got hung up this morning, but it looks like I still caught the two prettiest girls on the river."

"Hung up?" Kat asked innocently. No doubt he'd overslept or something. The guilty look he quickly hid made her nervous, but she didn't want to jump to conclusions.

"Never mind, I made it. Lilly, have you ever tried a kayak?" She shook her head, so he pointed to the gravel bar across the way. "Let's paddle over there and let you take it for a spin while we're in this slower water. What did you think of that waterfall back there?"

She only had eyes for Jake. "I was freaking out and hoping you'd come, and you did! Thanks, Jake... Dad."

When Lilly looked at her to see if it was okay to call him Dad, Kat wished she didn't feel possessive. She wanted to be a family, but admitted it had been nice having Lilly's affection mainly for herself. Jake was the show with his awesomeness.

"We were counting on you, Jake. Thanks for being here," Kat said. She would be grateful. "We were thinking of having a snack soon, so your timing is great." She angled the canoe toward the bank, feeling the resistance of the water against the paddle as she wondered what Jake was up to.

He couldn't fool Kat—she knew he was hiding something. She prayed it wouldn't be something that would crush the heart of his newest fan club member.

As time ticked by, Kat felt envy gnawing at her. Jake and Lilly spent the rest of the trip in the canoe, and he taught her paddling basics and how to slide up close to sunning turtles or spy on fish. Kat tagged along in the kayak.

They were paddling all over, just jabbering their heads off, and Kat desperately needed shore and aspirin. She felt honest to goodness tears of relief when they reached the takeout at Falls Mill.

Jake and Lilly still hadn't pulled in next to her—he was teaching her how to make loud smacking sounds by hitting her paddle flat on the water's surface in the last slow water, but Kat was done. The shrieking laughter combined with the smacking had her almost running for the Clubhouse.

She would let Lana know they survived and collect her truck

from the parking area. A hot shower, maybe lay down before supper... With one more glance at her roustabouts making their way slowly to the landing, she stepped into the timeless building.

"Kat, my dear. I've been dying of curiosity since Jake raced in here for a shuttle a few hours ago. I hadn't heard he was back in town."

"Well, he is," Kat snapped, then immediately apologized when she saw the look on the gentle, white-haired lady's lined face. "I'm sorry for being short, Emily. It was a long float and I think I might have gotten a little too much sun."

"You look a little worse for the wear, hon." Emily glanced across the way toward the landing with a sympathetic look.

"It's none of my business, anyway. I'm covering the front desk today for the kids and it was unexpected excitement. Speaking of excitement, Lana and Garrett went to Crestview to pick up the baby's crib. I'm so excited. It was handmade." Garrett's sweet grandma was trying to change the subject to let her off easy.

"No, of course everyone will be curious. Jake says he's back to stay." Kat sighed. "Apparently, he's re-opening the Hitchin' Post. He'll be living out at the ranch, I guess."

"So ya'll are going to make a go of it? I heard through the grapevine you'd been out to see Tom about a divorce and he couldn't talk you out of it. I do believe that young man would make me change my mind."

Emily gave Kat a speculative look. "The feed store, huh? Well, we sure could use the place open. Several more of our stores, really. It's a pain to go all the way to Crestview sometimes. I'm curious if the old folks in this town will do business with Jake again after the way he left last time. He left Hank in a lurch, and lots of folks were hard on your parents because he and Jaime weren't here to take their share of the heat..."

The voice in the doorway cut her off. "G'day, Missus Wilcox. Kat, mind throwing me the keys? Lilly and I will load up while you ladies finish your storytelling."

Emily had the grace to look embarrassed, and Kat knew she

was. She tossed him the keys. She shouldn't have been gossiping. It only added fuel to rumors, and it was best just to lie low until they figured out what was going on.

Kat could've used Lana's counsel, and it surprised her Lana hadn't told her about the crib. Or had she? Kat was a hot mess.

"Good luck, honey, on the man and the adoption." Emily patted her arm.

"Thank you. I can't believe how perfectly Lilly is fitting in," Kat said, glad to change the subject.

"Eli mentioned she was an angel. Warms my heart. There are few responsibilities greater than raising children to be kind, responsible, and principled. I am grateful every day I had the chance to raise a child. It didn't unfold as I had imagined, but it was a genuinely blessed time for Jasper and me. And now, Garrett is making us great-grandparents. It feels like quite an achievement for these old bones."

She patted her perfect white bun and nodded at Kat to run along. "Asking for help when you need it shows strength, not weakness. Sometimes a leap of faith and a little luck is all you need. Run on and get some rest, sweetie."

"Thanks, Emily." With a warm smile and a wave, Kat added, "I suspect we'll need the luck."

She found her crew loading the cooler onto her tailgate, and though they were still teasing each other, Jake was pointedly ignoring her. He hated it when people gossiped about him and would hold a grudge.

"Darn it all," she muttered, feeling defeated.

"Mom, can I ride in the back of the truck on the way home?" Kat's initial resistance weakened when she saw the genuine, pleading expression on Lilly's face, which resembled that of a perfectly well-adjusted child about to beg.

As she struggled to find a compromise, Jake said, "How about if we both ride in the back and we promise to keep our hands and feet inside the vehicle at all times?"

Kat sighed. Looked like she was taking the dirt road home slowly, so the kids could have fun while she acted like the grownup. Suddenly, Kat felt ancient. How come she never thought of the fun things to do?

Had she really turned into an old lady?

Sure thing.

"Lilly, you can't ride in the back of the truck because of seat belt laws, but if you sit here on the spare tire, and listen to Jake, we'll bend the rules a bit. Keep your hands in, okay?"

A thrill passed over Lilly's face, and she looked to be in absolute heaven when Jake swung the child into the back. He threw a towel at Lilly, instructing her to lay it over the tire to make a more comfortable seat. He closed the tailgate and hopped in the back with her.

Kat couldn't help but desire Jake, even if she felt left out. In his cutoff blue jeans and sleeveless tee, he looked so yummy—if only... Making sure Lilly was safe, Kat climbed into the cab and felt more alone than ever, despite her chance for a family.

They'd made plans to meet Jake at the feed store the next afternoon, and Kat's stomach twisted with anxiety despite Lilly's excitement. He was standing out front when they pulled up.

"Hey, pumpkin, glad my girls could make it." He ruffled Lilly's hair and placed a lazy kiss on Kat's cheek. "So, what do you think?"

He spread his arms wide, showcasing the storefront, and Kat wondered what she'd agreed to. The store looked deserted and dirty, like many of the other businesses, a long way from the store it had once been.

The sidewalk suddenly wasn't empty anymore as Vivian Reed, the resident cougar of Riverbend Falls, strolled up it with an eye on Jake.

"Jakob Summers. I heard through the grapevine you roared back in to town, causing a ruckus already. You bought Hanks. Bold move, young man, my hats off to you. Are you thinking of running the store on your own?"

Kat noticed the doubt etched on her face, and Jake's body language showed he was up for the challenge.

"Miss Vivian, I appreciate your excitement." He stepped out into the deserted street, the only thing breaking the silence was his voice calling back, "Actually, I'd appreciate if you'd support me at the next town council meeting when I suggest a renovation project for Riverbend Falls's Main Street."

After doing a little spin, he sauntered back to where the ladies were standing. As the realization sunk in that he wasn't joking, Kat and Vivian exchanged stunned looks. Jake had lost his mind. To take on such a project, one would need to invest a colossal amount of personal time.

"I don't intend to run the store myself all by myself, though. Kat will keep me in line."

He grinned at Kat, and she choked. He had just cheerfully put their social life in the clutches of the town's womenfolk, who were notorious for their nosiness. She was certain that if she gave them an inch with their henpecking ways, they would break her like a greenie.

"Jake, really—" Kat tried, but Vivian, looking like the house cat who just ate the family finch, interrupted her ever so graciously.

"Well, well. I must run along, lots of work to do. I'll leave you to your planning. Interesting. A renovation of Main Street, hmmm. I find the idea captivating." With a fond pat on Kat's arm, Vivian hurried away.

"You know she's going to spread that notion like wildfire throughout the town. What were you thinking?" Kat looked at Lilly, who was listening interestedly, and she changed the subject.

"For now, oh superhero of mine, how are you planning to turn this," Kat gestured at the grimy building and barn, "into a business—let alone a thriving one on your pretty new Main Street?"

At least she tried to switch gears. Jake compelled her to be insulting.

"Ye, of little faith. Ladies, dream with me a minute." Lilly giggled and took his outstretched hand as he held the door open. Kat followed with a sigh.

Sometimes, when life gave you everything you ever wanted, you had to ask yourself why you wanted so much.

At dinner that night, Jake tried hard to be extra affable to Eli. He knew he'd been needling the old man since he arrived, but he'd resented the guardian's unending devotion to Kat. She could do no wrong in his eyes.

Eli had always been fond of Jake, but hadn't forgiven him for eloping with his granddaughter. Jake mentioned to Eli yesterday morning that they were family, and they should learn to tolerate each other, and it had resulted in a bit of a truce.

He felt strangely at home as he looked around the table. The idea of caring for a child had always intimidated him, but Lilly's maturity and composure put him at ease. She kept impressing him with her sharp questions. And Kat wouldn't try to get pregnant again. That... well, thank the heavens Kat had figured another way to have her heart's desire.

"I'll help with the dishes," Jake said. He could get used to this routine stuff. Lilly and Eli had gone to the living room to watch TV, and he figured dishwashing time might be a fun time to work in some kissing.

Kat had agreed to let him stay in the bedroom across the hall from hers, but she'd been adamant about needing their own space. He figured it wouldn't be long, and she'd come to him.

"You crazy freak, are you nuts?" Kat wheeled on him as soon as he entered the kitchen.

"Whoa, babe, what's your deal?" He held up one hand and looked for a spot to set the dishes down he was carrying. When a filly kicks, you need to be mobile. "You don't want my help, or what?"

"Dad gum right, you're gonna help. You come waltzing in, dumping your schemes on me, you—"

"Language, mom..." he interrupted, hoping she'd keep her voice down. It sort of worked, but her quieter voice was still venom soaked.

"Main Street renovation project? That was not part of the deal. Where does that even come from, anyway? Who's going to coordinate... I have a child to look after, remember? Thanks to you, I have to divide my precious time with her and my horses to help you pretend to run a business that you won't last a month at."

"Hey, tighten up." Jake was getting aggravated. Where did she come off yelling at him for offering to invest his time to make something better? It was exactly the stunts she'd pulled all along.

"The renovation was my idea. I wasn't asking for your help with it, just with the store, and not a lot, so stop spewing vitriol. Have you checked your blood sugar lately? You're acting out of sorts."

She glared at him. "For your information, it's a little low and I have a doctor's appointment tomorrow. I know how to take care of myself, and I'm not out of sorts. I'm aggravated at you for charging in here and changing everything. Life was fine."

"Well, too bad, princess. This is my family, too, and things are changing. You better get used to it." He gestured at the dishes he'd ditched on the island. "I think I'll rescind my offer of help, though. I'd hate for you to go off on me because I helped with the chores. Good night."

He said his good nights to Lilly and Eli before climbing the stairs to the room that was his and firmly shut the door

Why did she have to get so insane sometimes? He knew her diabetes gave her blood sugar spikes, but Kat was such a beautiful, warm, thoughtful girl. Hard to believe the two personalities could exist in the same woman.

But she was his wife, and he loved her for all her complexities. He'd win her over. Heck, he'd thought the idea would make her happy. Women! Never could tell what was gonna put a bee in their bonnet.

Well, Kat may not want him, and she was the only person in the world who stayed crazy mad at him, but if there was anything Jake was good at it, it was beating the odds. He was ready for this. She'd come around.

Jake settled into his chair and reached for his laptop, the cool metal casing feeling familiar in his hands. Since discovering it as an alternative to paperwork, he'd become much more efficient.

He'd been using software to prep schedules and track

salaries for a couple of years now. He planned to use his skills for this new venture. Jake leaned back in his chair, studying the plans he'd been making for the last few days with a critical eye.

He was eager to take on the challenge of the feed store and he hoped the changes he had in mind would get him some street credit rather than thrown out on his backside. But it should work.

Yesterday, he got caught up with Eli working on the fence that Ragland had started earlier. Eli ran Ragland off for sleeping in his truck. That had made Jake late to meet the girls, but Eli had filled Jake in on the lay of the land, and the opportunity to literally mend fences with the old man had been too good to pass up.

He'd called Hank, who kindly told him where all Mary's bookkeeping notes had been carefully stored, and they'd been there. He reviewed them, noticing the last decade sales slowly dwindle as ranchers sold down their herds to keep their ranches.

An ice storm had nearly crippled the revenue when several of the younger ranchers sold their places and moved their families to the city to earn a living. He could see the dip to correspond to what Kat had told him about the ice storm.

He'd been in Texas and couldn't picture the devastation she'd described. It near to broke her when her wild horses were killed. She found her favorite stallion with an ice dagger through his head and three others shot. They ruled the shootings a hunting accident since it was deer season, but no one believed it. She'd suspected old man Ragland, so why she'd let his son work for her, he didn't know.

He hung his head.

I should've been here.

She'd carried the sorrow and blamed herself for not doing more, while making sure the rest of the herd stayed safe. He loved his wife's spirit. If she could find a little corner in that big heart of hers for him...

No matter. She was his girl, and he wasn't turning her loose.

He'd bought a business in a ghost town.

There was a fix for that, though. He needed to make beef

more profitable, or he wouldn't have anyone left to sell grain to.

Eli had given him some real nuggets to focus on for the feed store. He needed to talk to his twin, because it seemed she had her hands in a pie he wanted a piece of. Seemed the resort had some unfilled needs, and he had an idea how to fill them.

He did a little online shopping, looking at greenhouse supplies and beef freezers while his mind worked on a more pressing problem. How to make the Main Street project appealing to Kat? There was no way he could pull that off by himself.

There'd be all those women to deal with.

Surely it wouldn't be that big of a deal if everyone just shined up their places a bit. He turned back to his laptop and the depressed agriculture numbers posted earlier that day.

Jake knew he needed to take the leap and start with his own business. He'd have the barn painted and fresh signs made. The windows could stay. He envisioned a younger Kat staring at the rodeo posters in that window, giving him an opportunity to admire her incognito. Yeah, he'd keep the old vintage store windows and work with them, though he was being ridiculously sentimental.

Jake closed the computer and kicked off his shoes. He threw himself onto the bed, the softness of the blankets a slight comfort as he let out a sigh of frustration. Lying so close to Kat and not having her under his arm was disturbing. His mind was so preoccupied that even the quietness of the house couldn't lull him to sleep, and he lay awake for what felt like hours.

Chapter 5

The next day was a Monday, all day. She had a raging headache. Lilly didn't want to go to school. Jake was up and gone before daylight and hadn't left a note or any sign of where he was. She'd rather be hogtied than call him to fix her flat. Eli would be out riding fence lines since Park didn't show.

Kat had to pull it together.

"I don't want to go," Lilly said. "Can't I stay home and help you?"

Kat was tempted, just for time to bond, but she shook her head. She'd finished fixing her flat tire, and Lilly had at least come out the door on her own.

"I've got an idea. Don't you have show-and-tell today?" Kat asked.

"Yeah, but I don't have anything special to take." Lilly glanced at her, and Kat pulled out the arrowhead she found yesterday evening.

"How about this? Found right here on our riverbank." Kat hoped the cleverly whittled rock would be enough to elicit interest from a 6-year-old.

Lilly reached out for the arrowhead and gave it a good looking over. "Okay, cool. Thanks. I better hurry. Here comes the bus."

The kid had something on her mind, but she left smiling.

The new gelding, Mr. No Name, had wandered bravely out into the corral and was nibbling at a hay feeder. Good for him! She fed the other horses and checked on Potato Chip. At least the horse seemed better today, but there was something bugging her. Something out of place she just couldn't put her finger on.

She fed Dream a carrot and gave him a hug, then cleaned up and headed out to her appointment with Doc Robbins. The waiting room of his small practice was cozy and inviting, with equine art adorning the walls.

Kat usually found the space to be a calming oasis. Not today. Minor details were setting her off, and she was becoming easily agitated.

If she didn't feel up to it after her doctor's appointment, Kat decided she would put off grocery shopping until she felt better. The grocery store was next to Vivian's office, and Kat felt it might be smart to avoid the clever lady for the time being.

Hmm... homemade pizza sounded good. She could pull that together with what she had on hand.

"Kat?"

Doc Robbins was a handsome older man and very easygoing. He'd been treating her since she was a little girl. Her type two diabetes was mild, but it made her a regular customer, as he liked to tease. He looked concerned, and her stomach fluttered. Humor was her go to.

"Don't look so glum, Doc. What's up? Am I dying?"

"Well, let's hope not. You're going to have a baby."

He noticed the shock and terror that coursed through her.

"I can see you're surprised. I know we discussed the fact that having a baby poses a risk for you. Can I ask if you've been keeping up with your birth control routine?"

"I stopped having sex so..."

"So, this baby was conceived without sex?" He had a somewhat skeptical expression on his face, accompanied by a gentle smile, which was part of what made him so charming.

She lowered her head and closed her eyes, reliving the intimate moment when the baby inside her was created. The mere thought of what Jake would say made her cringe. She lifted her head, and the tears brimmed over, spilling down her cheeks.

"Don't worry, kiddo. It can be done. You'll have to change your lifestyle."

"Oh, Doc! I..." She stood up, having dressed while waiting for her results. "I better get going."

"I'll see you every two weeks. If you're certain about accepting the risk that you may not carry the baby full term."

"I'm sure, Doc. I'll take the chance. No question." Her voice trembled.

"At the risk of interfering, I heard Jake was in town. I'm guessing he's the father and you're not sure what he's going to say. I think you should give him a chance, Kat. His heart's in the right place."

"You think he can accept the news? He's going to be a father. I'm pregnant. Oh flippin' frig." She felt despair closing over her. Jake would think she did it on purpose.

Doc Robbins ducked his head, letting her know he hoped Jake would accept it. "Take care of yourself, Kat. I'll see you in two weeks."

He patted her shoulder, clearly hoping to comfort her. The warmth of the office seemed to evaporate as Kat left, the cold reality of the situation settling in.

When she got home, she started toward the attic. It was unused—full of the past. This was punishment. She was going to pull out the things she'd bought for Melody, the baby they lost.

A bout of nausea hit and she wondered if it was morning sickness—or unspent grief. She changed her mind about the baby clothes and chose saltines and tea in the kitchen instead. There would be a million things she'd have to do. Starting with telling Jake.

One thing at a time...

She crunched the crackers with determination, trying to calm herself. Putting the tea water on to boil, she realized she was boxed in. Everything would change. Again. The small amount of trust they'd been building the past few days as they struggled to be together again would evaporate when he realized she hadn't been taking her birth control when she came to him.

She'd threatened to get pregnant alone before and with the divorce paper thing—this was going to look bad.

She'd make him breakfast tomorrow and tell him. What would he say?

There was a time when they were deeply in love and excited about starting a family. That period of her life was priceless to her. They both carried the pain of the miscarriage, and their attempts to talk about it always ended in regret. Eventually, they'd agreed to not bring it up again. It had been the only way to move on.

Now... well, they'd have to talk. Jake wasn't going to be able to stonewall her again. He was going to be mad, though, and talking him down was going to be harder than poking a cat from under the front porch with a rope.

Turned out she had plenty of time to worry. He didn't come for dinner, but Eli came in and said not to wait up for Jake. He wouldn't be home until late.

At dinner, she tried to keep up a light banter over the pizza she'd made, but it was no use. Jake's absence was a huge downer for them. Such a brief time it had taken him to become the shining light in their lives. She felt alone, more so than she had before he came. To have him so close and not have him...

She realized she could manage without him, but for the sake of Lilly and her baby, she wanted to build a family more than anything else. Though he wasn't always reliable, he had a way of making them feel special with his promises and attention.

Some of Jake was better than none.

Lying in bed across from Jake's room that night, Kat cried buckets, wishing for the special closeness they shared in the early years.

Dread made her cry harder when she thought if something went wrong this time, she would leave Lilly and Jake both. Finally, exhaustion beat her and she collapsed into a deep sleep, tears drying on her cheeks.

She slipped downstairs the next morning, determined to get the truth out. By six-thirty, the kitchen smelled of bacon, sausage, French toast, and her special recipe cornbread she'd put together to sweeten up the men.

The kitchen was silent until Eli, Jake, and Lilly all arrived at the same time—Eli through the back door, and Jake and Lilly through the kitchen's swinging door. Then suddenly the room was full of chatter and the smell of breakfast cooking.

Kat grinned. "Aha, ya'll smelled the grub, eh? I've been slaving away, hoping for a good, hungry mess of cowhands to pile in."

Lilly giggled and Eli cleared his throat, saying, "Uh, well, I was fixing to take off on my morning ride when I noticed you were bustling around in here. Be a shame to waste a hot breakfast."

"It sure would. I'm awful glad you finally learned to cook, Kat." Jake pulled the kitchen chair out for Lilly before settling himself in and told her, "Yep, your mom couldn't cook a lick when I met her."

"It's a wonder I learned to boil water, living in that trailer. I don't know how we ever agreed that a convection oven—and a hotplate—was a kitchen." She chuckled. "It was fun, though. I don't begrudge the experience, but I'm mighty happy to have this big ole kitchen to putter around in."

"Me, too," said Lilly as she poured a pile of syrup on her plate, drowning her bacon and toast. "I'm going to learn to cook like you, Mom. Will you teach me to make pies, too?"

"You bet, kiddo. Now everybody eat up. Lilly, you still have to get ready for school. The school bus will be here in no time."

As they ate, Lilly told cute stories about yesterday's show-and-tell, but Kat couldn't concentrate.

She was relieved when Lilly and Eli were each bundled off in their respective directions, though she wanted to run as well, to keep her secret to herself. She hated to ruin the warm feeling of family that had been in the kitchen that morning.

"Can I have some more of that coffee?" Jake asked.

She poured him a cup, knowing he was not functional until

he'd consumed at least a pot of black coffee, a habit they used to share. "You might as well sit down. I've got something I need to talk to you about."

"Let's forget the talking and fool around instead."

The desire in his husky voice triggered the memory of his powerful hands on her soft skin when... shoot. When they'd made this baby.

"Hardly," she responded, cursing the immediate quiver in her voice. "We've covered this. I don't want to confuse things for Lilly..."

"She's not here, Kat. Are you sure you're not afraid you're the one who doesn't want to be confused?"

He wrapped his arms around her and she rested in them briefly before pulling away. She sat across the table from him.

He sat, looking around. "You did a respectable job remodeling this place. I like this room. Makes me want to sit around the table like the Waltons."

Kat looked at him, trying to decide if he was mocking her, but he seemed sincere, and she relaxed marginally, hoping for the best. Kat realized this was the now or never moment. Time to find out how Jake felt about finding out she was carrying his baby.

"Thanks. The Waltons were a pretty full family." She hesitated. Her silence was so prolonged, Jake finally looked at her close, trying to figure out what was bothering her.

"What's up, babe?"

Kat's heart was racing, and the blood rushed to her face. Her hands were shaking, and she wasn't sure, but as she wiped her damp palms on her knees, she thought they were shaking too. She felt like throwing up. This time, she knew it had nothing to do with her morning sickness. This was pure dread.

"I need to talk to you about something serious."

He smiled at her, but he looked wary. "This isn't a ploy to get rid of me, is it?"

His blue eyes looked deep into her own and she felt his spike of concern, knew it as well as she knew herself. They were once so deeply in love that they could only see each other and not the world around them. Before they lost the baby...

"Perhaps. I want you to stay, Jake. What I'm going to tell you doesn't change the fact I think it's unhealthy for us, this imaginary relationship we're working so hard at—but I want you to stay. It's something... well, shoot, Jake. You don't want to hear it."

She put her head in her hands and felt the sting of tears burning her eyes. Emotional storms kept spinning up out of nowhere, and it was driving her nuts.

He stood, coming around the table, and put his hands on her shoulders. "What is it, my moon goddess? If we work together, we can tackle any problem. What's wrong?"

She straightened up, taking strength from his words. "I'm pregnant."

He recoiled as if she had stung him. A mixture of shock, fear, and anger played across his face. He quickly replaced his anger with a blank look, the kind he had perfected over the years to hide his actual feelings.

"Pregnant?" As he walked toward her herb window, he said the word, sounding as though she had confessed to having a contagious disease.

Knowing what was next, she steeled herself. The weight of his disappointment was heavy on her shoulders as she braced herself for his outburst. That's just how it was. She was ready to withstand any kind of verbal assault he wanted to throw at her. As soon as he realized how determined she was, he'd back away, preferring a life without complication.

As he turned from the window, his eyes met hers and she saw the pain etched on his face, making her want to reach out and comfort him.

He held up his hand to stop her. A chilly frost emanated from him and he walked past her without a word. A moment later, she heard the front door slam, and she moved to the window to watch him kick his way up the gravel drive to the dirt road.

Eli's dog, Lucky, followed behind at a cautious distance. He hadn't taken his stuff, so he'd be back, but she'd seen it in his eyes. Disgust. She let the tears fall freely as she walked in a daze to the kitchen.

"It's for the best. Not meant to be." She whispered the mantra, willing it to be true as she splashed her face, emptied her guts, and splashed her face again. She wished she wore make-up so she could hide her red-rimmed eyes.

Nothing had changed with Jake. His attitude was the same, despite how he'd been acting with Lilly. Now he knew everything, and when they called it quits this time, she could know for sure he'd be gone for good.

Furious with his wife, it was the betrayal that hurt the worst. She must have known she was pregnant, and that's why she wanted a divorce.

It was probably that blamed cowboy! He'd seen the way he looked at Kat, like he could taste her. Made his blood run hot. He didn't trust Park Ragland or his father any further than he could spit. Jake charged up the gravel road, intent on burning off his fury. He should have broken his nose.

What was Kat thinking? Fine, she had an indiscretion. He hadn't been tending to her needs, and she'd always been a passionate woman. But having a baby could kill her. Did the jerk know his seed could very well end the life of one of the most caring people on earth?

Jake was all too familiar with it. He couldn't shake the guilt he felt for his part in what almost cost Kat her life before. She knew she had to keep using birth control for her well-being.

In the beginning, they'd been foolishly excited and begun picking out names. Melody for a girl, and if it was a boy, Andrew. Then it was all gone.

She'd been a wilted flower when he stumbled upon her, collapsed on the floor in a heap of blood. Anger consumed him, blaming himself, her, and the universe for the unfairness of it all. The idea of losing Kat left him feeling hollow.

That Kat was unaware of her own survival haunted Jake.

She pulled away, into herself, and lost interest, and Jake's attempts to cheer her up fell short. Kat abandoned her passion for photography, uninterested in capturing the rodeos, and preferred to relax in the trailer. She had created a cozy cocoon for herself by piling blankets and pillows on the couch and rarely left for months.

His twin came and tried to help, but the girls ended up arguing fiercely. And then Kat woke up. Sort of. She started showering and getting dressed, but was angry with him. She sent passive aggressive barbs his way... Jake didn't know how to reach Kat, the real her behind the glossy surface.

After some time, she began to hang around the circuit again, chatting up the cowboys, even if it was just for innocent conversation. Despite Jake's lack of dancing skills, he took her to dance often, content to watch her laugh and have fun with everyone else.

He let her do what she wanted—just grateful she'd stopped rocking quietly in the dark. He couldn't shake off the guilt that had consumed him after almost losing her. She'd left him all alone with nothing but his thoughts for company. He took chances, pushing the limits of his and his horse's endurance, all hoping to catch her eye.

And then Kat went all out to seduce him. Often. It was great. Man, they'd always had a fantastic sex life, but Kat still felt closed off emotionally, so it just got weird. While he was trying to find clean sheets to surprise her, he found her stash of birth control pills.

He asked her about them and she was like, "I'm giving it another go." It was as if the memories of the struggles they faced to save her had slipped from her mind. She was willing to throw it all away, and the pain of it lingered.

He kicked a rock as he continued to walk down the dirt road. He was alone in the middle of nowhere, surrounded by towering trees alight with the vibrant colors of fall. If only he could appreciate it instead of feeling so dreadfully alone.

Not alone, after all. Eli's Australian Shepherd was lurking around behind him. He saw a big rock and sat on it. The chill seeping through his jeans was barely noticeable as he considered the chill in his soul. After a while, the dog came and lay down at his feet. As he stroked the dog's silky ears, he wondered what to do now?

Walk? Fight for her? What if she had fallen for someone else? Too bad. They were in it together for the long haul. He remembered how she'd stuck to his side when he'd been thrown. His own trusted horse, the owner of the hooves that nearly broke his back. He'd been in the hospital for two months and Kat had come every day, encouraging him, making him laugh.

She was the old Kat those days, but when he'd left the hospital, things were different. It seemed like she had retreated further into herself, making conversation nearly impossible.

When she'd come back to Riverbend Falls to run her ranch, they'd barely been speaking, though there was little animosity, just... existing. Well, they'd grown apart, so what? He would fix it. But raising another man's baby? Another thought raised hopefully and dreadfully in his mind all at the same time.

What if it wasn't another man's baby? She couldn't be three months yet. Her long frame only showed a hint of stomach, which he'd idly been wondering how she was achieving since she ate like a mouse.

What if the baby was his? The hope that his wife had been faithful was uplifting, but if she lost the baby, or worse, he lost Kat—he didn't know how life could go on for him... What if his seed killed the woman he loved because for the second time in their twelve-year marriage, he'd been a careless husband?

With a frustrated groan, he stood, trying to decide what to do. He turned toward Kat's presence.

Her song called him more soundly than the rodeo, and he wished it had only been two times that he'd been careless with the woman he loved. He prayed it wasn't too late for them, no matter what the future held.

Chapter 6

Low on supplies, with Jake off sulking, Kat went shopping. Halloween was approaching, and she was planning to throw a party for Lilly hoping to help her make friends. She hurried and was able to pick Lilly up before she got on the bus at school, so Eli had taken her on the trail for a riding lesson.

She stood in the kitchen humming an out of tune fifties ditty, filling canisters with flour and sugar when she experienced a little head rush. Kat grabbed the counter and held on, mostly to keep her feet under her. When she felt steady, she moved to the barstool, a hot spike of fear flushing her skin with heat.

Her head snapped up when she heard the front door open, and a second later Jake was standing in front of her, glowering ferociously.

"I'm fine," she said, feeling certain he must know somehow that she'd nearly fainted. His glare deepened, and she cringed, shifting her attention to a deep stain in the tabletop where once long ago a too-hot pan had been placed there. It was special, and she'd kept the table when she remodeled for sentimental reasons. Idly, she traced the scar, waiting for the yelling to start.

"Is the baby mine?"

The quiet question stunned her. "Of course it's yours, you jerk!" She'd never cheated on him. That he could wonder if she had incensed her.

He sat across from her, but his voice was ice. "I'm the jerk?

You show up after two years to divorce me, use me for sex, knowing plenty good and well how I feel... were you taking your birth control?"

"Yes... not faithfully." Her voice was quieter. She knew he would make it look as if she tricked him on purpose.

"So, when you held me to you that last time, you knew you weren't on the pill? I knew it!" He slammed his hand down on the counter. "Geez, Kat, it almost destroyed us the last time you got pregnant! You planned to do it again and divorce me while playing Russian roulette with your life—you wouldn't even have told me we made a baby, would you?"

He shook his head, disgusted. "Then there was Lilly. You met her on the way home, then you needed me again. That's the long and short of it, am I right? The pieces finally fit."

"No." It was a whisper. "I didn't..."

"Oh, but you did Kat, you did."

He was spitting mad, and she dreaded what he might say next. He couldn't make her have an abortion. She wouldn't do it.

"Now here's the deal. You owe me, and I'm making my claim right now. You're taking a chance with the life of my child in there, too. Your selfish games are over now. Until that baby is born, I'm going to watch you like a hawk. You're gonna eat right, rest right, and from now until I hold our child in my arms, you're going to act like a proper wife in public."

"And in private?" Kat asked. "Where do we stand?"

"The birth of the baby is our priority, and we'll deal with divorce talk if we're still unable to move past our pettiness. It's not what I want, but I won't have my name dragged through the mud again because of your selfish whims."

"I'll agree to postponing any divorce talk," she grumbled. High handed but fair.

"What about Lilly?" He pulled his cap off, rubbing his hand through his hair briskly before pulling it back on like a knight donning his helmet before a battle. "You want to be a parent, Kat, well, you're gonna have to make that apparent to me, because all I see is the same little girl I married who's too busy running around saving everyone else—way too busy to commit to anything as serious as a family."

She exploded. "You're the freaking commitment-phobe. When was the last time you told me you loved me? I wonder if your desire for me is genuine or you just want me now because I said I was done. It's always the elusive chase for you."

She stood up, the sparks between them hot enough to bake biscuits. He growled her name, and it made the hair on her neck stand up. Then it dawned on her that he was offering to stay for good, and she could finally have the life she always wanted.

"But this is good," she said with a shake of her ponytail. "Jake, I hear you." With a joyful cry, she wrapped her arms around his neck, but he quickly stepped back, breaking the embrace. The ice was back in his voice and it swept through her.

"This is not good, Kat. Let me be more specific. I meant you'll be a good wife in public. I'm so disgusted with you right now, I can't think straight. You would have been content to hide my child from me, assuming you can slow down enough to carry a baby to full term. You'll be hard-pressed to get me to forgive for you this sham."

He left then, pushing through her swinging kitchen door back into the living room and fury filled her. Her howl echoed behind him, but she knew it would not bring Jake back. Whenever they argued about Melody, she felt like her heart was breaking into a million pieces, but he didn't seem to notice.

She despised him! She loved him! Desperate tears filled her eyes again.

Confused is what she was.

The sound of her cries echoed behind him, each one piercing his heart. He could never forget the soulful keening that marked the memory of the moment he had to tell his wife their baby girl was gone.

Kat's body, already six months pregnant, succumbed to the strain, leading to an internal hemorrhage. The doctor advised Jake and Kat to avoid pregnancy, quietly confiding to Jake that the emotional toll on Kat may be as deep as the physical scars she would carry.

Despite his suggestion, Kat had no interest in exploring counseling or adoption. Mistakenly thinking that time would heal Kat, Jake was content with her being alive. But the loss was still clearly dogging her, and what was he to do?

Now she seemed happier than she'd been in years. She was working hard to make a family, regardless of the danger to herself. He only wished she would have included him instead of going it alone.

But the risk was so great... Jake wondered wryly as he went back to his room if perhaps his own selfish pride might have not allowed her to heal... It was so hard for him to think about.

Kat was hard to figure, though. She wasn't the kind of girl who wanted to be given things—she needed to work for them. Well, she'd have her work cut out for her, carrying their baby, coaching him, and making a home for a sad little girl.

Maybe he could convince her to include him more—before they let time and bitterness edge out their precious memories... and if he couldn't, well, he'd fix it so something would help. Now to his other problem.

A few hours later, Jake closed his laptop.

He was way out of his league. Renovating the town. When Falls Mill was born in the spring, something happened that changed the motion in town, and the little revenues from tourism died.

How could they work together to build more for everyone? He stretched his hands behind his head, fingers interlocked, and considered his options.

He could just admit he was blowing smoke, but was he?

Jake remembered the lively town from his youth, and wanted to feel it again, even though things were different now. His view of it certainly was.

The businesses that weathered the storm deserved to be given the opportunity to thrive once more, but it seemed impossible for him to come up with a resolution that would make everyone happy.

Hmmm... Maybe he could coordinate a harvest festival with

Falls Mill for Main Street. He'd driven the short road to the Mill several times, hoping to see Jaime or Lana, but so far, he'd kept missing them. His sister was still avoiding Kat, obviously. Time to mend that.

If he threw the girls together on a project, their pride would make it happen, and then their true friendship would melt the barriers. He had to do everything.

It was a little short notice for this year, but they could reinvent the old fall festival. It could be all day long, with a street fair in town, and he could arrange regular hay ride shuttles that day from the feed store that hauled folks to town from the river and back with entertainment along the way.

They could sponsor a chili cook off in the park. Maybe he could get Falls Mill to take that. If he could talk the shopkeepers into having sidewalk sales to catch people's attentions on the way...

He bet his folks would help. Then they'd have to talk, too. He would ask Kat what she thought about...

It seemed like a daunting task to put on a woman who was expecting. He wished he hadn't asked Kat for her help with the store, she had so much on her plate.

Jake had been thinking about asking his mom what she thought about hiring on to help at the register a few times a week. It appeared she had reinvented herself as well, and fancied herself a social influencer. He thought she might enjoy what he intended to be a nice hub for gossip. And sales.

He would ask Tabby then, he decided. He would need Kat, too, but he didn't think she would limit her activity, and she was going to have to. Sometimes her independence was a pain. He was going to have to distract her and keep her busy doing something light but worthwhile.

Standing up, he thought it was the perfect moment to set some ground rules. Kat had plenty of time to cool down. It was likely that she had already written a dozen rules on two separate lists.

The woman could organize a basket of kittens... though this time dealing with her was liable to feel more like sorting bobcats.

She was sitting at the island, her head down in her arms. Unless he was mistaken, she hadn't moved. There was a slew of groceries all around her, an inordinate amount of shopping. Sacks of Halloween candy and supplies were mixed with industrial sized containers of peanut butter and pickles and random food stuff.

"Kat, babe?"

She lifted her head and her expression frightened him.

What if the baby was already proving to be too much for her? She was white as a sheet. He crossed to her and wrapped his arms around her stiff figure.

She remained rigid for a moment, then laughter bubbled from her lips. Despite the sound, her eyes were blank. She had a problem with self-esteem, and Jake knew it.

Sometimes I'm denser than a forest.

He should've stayed with her after their argument. She was likely talking down to herself, feeling like nobody cared. He felt like a heel.

"Can we talk?" he asked.

Her laughter got louder, and he worried about her mental health. She hiccupped, and the laughter subsided.

"Lilly and Eli will be back soon," she said. "I have to put the groceries away."

A fake smile graced her soft lips as she hiccupped again.

She giggled as she surveyed the aftermath of the shopping frenzy around her. A saner sound, he noted thankfully. He pulled her to him for a quick hug, then released her, knowing she was using her "fake it 'til you make it" strategy to get herself together.

He put some space between them for his own sake as much as hers. His wife's sensuality was as potent as the day he married her, and he loved her more as the years rushed by.

They should've kept showing their love.

Looking for a distraction from his vital feelings for her, he glanced at her with raised eyebrows as his pinky hooked a pair of lacy black and orange underwear out of the bag filled with marshmallows. She snickered, and Jake's heart quickened at the thought of her wearing them.

She snatched the panties from his hand and gave him a playful swat with them.

"Dream on, handsome."

She looked around with clear eyes at the enormity of purchases on her counter, disbelief marred with humor.

"I think I might have gone a bit overboard on the shopping." The look she gave him conveyed her embarrassment. "I've been emotional lately..."

He raised both eyebrows at her in mock amusement. He was drawn to her, and he realized he needed her. How could he lend a hand without spooking her?

"May I assist the emotive mistress of Kindred Spirits Ranch in putting away these groceries?" He gave a pointed look at the pickles and grinned. "You get those bags, though. Looks like you might need to know where you put them."

She laughed. "Wow. I wonder what I left on Ralph's shelves? He probably thought I was nuts. Have you seen a bag of cashews?"

"Where *are* you going to put all this?" He waved at the two bags filled solely with pickles... sweet, dill, midges, and bread and butter slices. When he gave her a questioning look, she responded with a wry chuckle and answered his unspoken question.

"Yeah, pickle craving." She began sorting things into piles. "Some of this goes upstairs to my room, the baking stuff all goes on that counter, I'll put them away in the morning when I do my rolls for the Mill. Of course, milk and cereal, you know where they go but... all the Halloween and party stuff, frankly, I don't know yet. It's a little overwhelming."

He smirked as he located the matching bra in a bag with gummy bears. He handed her the cashews he found at the bottom. "Life is simply too dull without you in it, Kat. I have a plan. Let me tell you about it."

As they worked together to tidy up the kitchen, he marveled at how smoothly they worked together. He felt a wave of satisfaction wash over him as he surveyed his surroundings. He smiled to himself, realizing that his decision to come back had been the right one.

"What do you mean, no?"

It was the quiet of the night, and there stood Jake, six feet of deliciousness, in her bedroom doorway. If she said yes, there would be no turning back, and the warmth of Jake's embrace would be all she could think of.

"I said no, you can't come in." Kat pulled on her ponytail with an impatient gesture.

In the kitchen, they'd worked as a team to whip up a delicious supper of omelets and toast, with Lilly lending a helping hand.

As they worked together at the counter, the familiar routine of chopping and slicing cheese and leftover ham and peppers and onions brought back memories of similar meals they had made in Jake's small trailer, as she'd learned to cook.

Riverbend Falls held a special place in Kat's heart, and having him here now filled her with a sense of excitement and daring. If Jake weren't so stubborn, things would be easier.

To her, it seemed he ought to understand why she wasn't willing to sleep with him yet. Despite letting him into their lives, she still had to be cautious to prevent a broken heart.

As she thought about Jake's rodeo lifestyle, which she was starting to believe he'd left in his rearview, Kat couldn't help but dream of a future where he would settle down in her small town.

But he had a history of holding grudges, and it wasn't likely he'd forgiven her, yet. It wasn't his style to let things go easily. But if they rebuilt slowly...

She didn't like him invading her personal space. The line between what was actual and what wasn't became hazy. She shook her head again.

His easy features hardened, and Kat longed to stroke the stubble growing along his rigid jawline. She loved it when he got stubborn. It did something really sexy to his features.

"I'm your husband."

"Estranged husband who is challenging me to pretend we

are happy in public, but who has reminded me recently that there is a lot of anger simmering between us. We don't know what's going to happen." She softened her voice and could hear the plea in her tone. "Please..."

"Fine, have it your way, Kat." His ocean blue eyes held the same resolute determination as the stubborn set of his jaw. "You want me, though. I can taste it on your lips when we kiss." He tugged at his ball cap. "Don't leave without me in the morning. You always try to do too much. I know you're no lightweight, but you don't have to prove to me how tough you are. I believe you. We're going to limit the weight you tote, so you better get used to it."

Jake gestured impatiently, and Kat surrendered with a nod. He left her standing at the door to her room and walked into his own, closing the door firmly behind him.

She walked down the hall and looked in on Lilly. The girl was sleeping soundly, her dark hair sprayed against the orange bedding she'd chosen for her room. Kat dropped a kiss on Lilly's forehead and slipped back into her own room, moving to the window to look at the river in the distance.

She felt the familiar tug of affection for it, a passion she'd indulged in all her life. Eli used to tease her she'd been born part fish. Her scales were just invisible.

She smiled. Her grandfather was her rock, her friend. His age never slowed him down, and he'd taught Kat everything she knew about ranching. Despite the challenge of her difficult personality, he'd done a good job.

She was grateful for Eli's love and his lessons. He'd given her a family when she had none. Now she had a chance for a family of her own, and she was too afraid of the hole Jake would leave in her if the lure of the arena called him. She laid down and tried to sleep, but her bed felt desperately lonely.

The next morning, there was a light knock on her door. She pulled her robe on and opened the door to Jake, who strolled in looking amazingly awake for the hour.

"Heck of a room. No wonder you didn't want me in here. I

might never leave."

Jake walked around behind her and she caught her breath. She didn't want him in her room because then she'd never be able to be in it without thinking of him. How many times she'd longed for him beside her on the big oak bed.

Her room was a suite, really. A small dressing room with a wide entrance leading to her bed. A big walk-in bathroom with a glass shower.

"We forgot these downstairs yesterday," he said. "Didn't you say you wanted this stuff in your room?" He put bags containing underwear and deodorant and shampoo—enough for a small army—on the sitting-room table, then continued to look around. He was quiet, but she could see what he was thinking.

The room felt like a serene underwater oasis with its soft blue and green walls. Old sea charts and collections of seashells and netting covered the walls.

She even had the window portal converted into a fish tank, and in the small octagon space swam an iridescent beta fish. Kat knew the fish was exactly the color of Jake's eyes when passion crowded rational thought from his mind.

"It's like everything we talked about, Kat."

Wonder filled his words, and she wished she'd decorated the room in pink. She'd never wanted him to see this. He wouldn't believe she'd wanted to call it quits—she'd clearly built their dream room. She hadn't been planning to trap or trick him. She'd just accepted she'd have to enjoy it alone.

"Well, we talked about it for years. It figures I wouldn't have any originality decorating my place. But it changes nothing. This is my room, and I can't think with you in it. I still have a hard time accepting you're not just passing through and..."

She shrugged, pretending she hadn't built their dreamscape for him, but as a lark. She didn't think he was buying it, but it seemed he'd decided not to push. Shoving his hands in his pockets, he walked past where she stood near the door.

"I'll be working with you this morning. How long until you get around?"

She grinned, knowing he wasn't a morning person, or at least he hadn't been. "I'll head down and rustle us up some coffee."

"Are you going to wear that? I don't promise to keep my hands off you if I can't get that little scrap of a robe out of my mind."

She gave him a pointed look, willing herself not to grin. Gesturing firmly, she directed her gaze toward the door.

"I'll meet you downstairs," he said, his voice husky.

"See ya in a few," she agreed. He looked at the fish tank again with a calculating look, then pulled the door quietly behind him.

She smiled to herself as she moved to grab some jeans to tug on and it turned into laughter when she saw that somehow, in the short span of time he'd been in her room, he'd managed to lay the orange and black panties on her pillow.

Chapter 7

When he first showed up at her bedroom door, his wife was the tender girl he'd fallen in love with, but by the time he finished a few things in the barn and showed up in the kitchen, her protective shield was in place and she was bustling about, seeming to be irritated at him for being in her way.

She whisked together a sugar concoction for the cinnamon rolls that she'd just pulled from the oven. Jake rose from the stool where he'd been watching her with interest for the last bit and poured himself a third cup of coffee.

"Why do you make that stuff when you can't eat it?" He wondered whether she was wearing the underwear.

Make small talk.

He had no business thinking about what was under her Levis. Pregnant meant sex was off limits. It was making him grouchy.

"Money, honey," she joked. "This is a big pile of money that will turn into a small pile of grain."

She seemed comfortable in the enormous kitchen and he cursed himself for not seeing how badly she'd needed to... nest. Kat mostly hummed under her breath in the horrible off-key way she did, and even though he'd been determined to be cheerful when he woke up with the sun, his morning wasn't going well. She'd shut him out again.

His mood worsened as she poured herself a bowl of bran

and indicated with a nod toward the collection of sugary cereal boxes that he should choose.

He glanced at the pile of cinnamon rolls waiting to be iced.

"Why would I want cereal when I could have one of those?"

"These are for profit." She poured milk over her cereal and ate casually, leaning against the counter as she spooned up her breakfast.

Her smile didn't quite reach her eyes, and she seemed wary of him. He retrieved his own bowl and chose a cereal randomly, then put it back, realizing it was the healthy one she was eating. He looked longingly at the sweets, abandoning his bowl for his coffee cup.

"If you need special treatment..."

Her voice was syrupy, and he scowled deeper into his ceramic mug, enjoying the bittersweet flavor of the fresh ground coffee Kat was partial to. A far cry from the instant he'd been drinking the past several years, since she quit perking their morning brew.

"There's no need to be insensitive, Kat." He was pretty sure she'd cave and give him a cinnamon roll. "I want one of those, and I want extra frosting. Be a good girl and hook me up."

"They're already spoken for. I have two dozen for sale going to Falls Mill this morning."

Stubborn, but not willing to give in, he realized he was enjoying the banter. He missed talking with her, not just the melody of her voice, but the sure of herself attitude she brought to the conversation when she was feeling good about herself.

Smart and confident. It attracted him to her originally, though he'd soon discovered her bravado was a cover for the self-esteem issue. He'd spent years working to convince her she was every bit as wonderful as she pretended to the world she was. She was stubborn, but so was he.

"Have they already been sold?" Jake set down his mug and pulled out his wallet. "All of them?"

"Well, no. Lana's booked the Red Hat gals chapter meeting for coffee today and they requested a batch of my rolls. But Lana can usually sell them to the last one."

She gave him one of those looks, the look that said he wasn't likely to win, and he felt a rush at the challenge. Man, she was beautiful, her black hair tied back in a braid and a smudge of flour across her nose.

"Great. How much are they?"

"She sells them for four dollars apiece."

"Four dollars each?" He goggled at the stack. "They must be pretty freaking good. What's your cut?"

"They're good," she said, looking down her nose, "and I get 50 percent."

He placed a hundred-dollar bill on the counter and picked up one roll off the cooling stack. Jake stepped around beside her, holding her gaze until he heard her breathing pick up. He was stoked that just being near her still turned her on after all these years.

Stroked a man's ego, if nothing else.

With an exaggerated flare, he reached for the frosting bowl.

"What are you doing?"

Her throaty voice was pitched low, and he stared into her dark eyes, wondering what she was thinking. Man, he sure hoped she was thinking what he was thinking.

Stop thinking about sex.

He grabbed the spatula and moved behind her. He slid his arms around her and placed the spatula in her hand, his hands resting loosely atop hers.

"Getting my first hands-on lesson in frosting expensive cinnamon rolls. Show me how, then. I'll frost mine while you do the rest of the batch I'm buying for the... what did you call them—red hats? You're making a killing on these. I want to taste one."

She nodded, but barely. "Jake—"

"Definitely have to taste this now..."

He kissed her neck then, the way he'd wanted to since he walked into the room and saw the luscious exposed skin. Jake indulged just long enough to feel her tremble, then stopped the whisper light kisses.

He was barely controlling the urge to ravish her right on the kitchen floor. He wanted her, but he had to keep his hands off her. Jake backed off just a smidge. The sound of her distressed breathing was a sign that she wasn't ready. Not yet.

Her body betrayed her, and she knew it. He was tempting her like a brood mare in heat. Their love making was never the hitch, it was the lack of communication between them that had become so obvious by the choices they made in their lives. Jake wanted action—she wanted love.

She wanted to throw him on the floor and let him make the earth move for her. She knew he could. He never failed to. He said she disgusted him, yet... the way he touched her reverently said the words his mouth wasn't saying.

Why was he here, being so nice to her? Was he really hoping to rekindle their love?

Maybe her annoying levels of self-doubt were getting the best of her and she wasn't giving Jake the chance he deserved. She went to him that night, certain that their relationship was about to end, but instead of ending things, she spent one more night tangled in his sheets.

The presence of Lilly and the baby shifted her perspective. Would she be seeking change otherwise? The rancher's life she'd accepted demanded responsibility, which clashed with Jake's nature. If Lilly hadn't been here, with Kat just making a mess of things, would Jake have stuck around?

No way, he would've tried to persuade her to go back with him. But he said he'd sold the trailer and... why couldn't she just believe in him?

"Earth to moon goddess. Are you going to show me how to do this, or should I just dip mine in?" He waved the pastry over the frosting bowl like a spoon. "I'm eating this."

The memory of the first time Jake called her that brought a fond smile to her lips. The moon had been full, illuminating the streets of San Antonio on the night that their hearts overflowed with emotion.

She'd still been pregnant with Melody, and they were sitting in a quiet arena the night before one of Jake's big events. They'd talked about settling down once Jake finished the season.

Not sure where they'd move, they'd talked of every option but coming home. Wherever it was would have a room designed to soothe the way the river did.

Well, she'd still designed her room the way they dreamed of, but everything else had been a wash. Losing the baby changed the way they talked about everything. Kat shook her head and focused.

"I'm with ya. Like this." She guided his hand holding the cinnamon roll over the counter and put a heavy dollop of the frosting on it. She handed him the spatula, and as he watched, she guided his hand to recreate the perfect swirl of the bread.

"That's my secret," she said. The intensity of the moment made it difficult for her to catch her breath. "Make it pretty. Since I don't get to eat them, that's where I find my glee."

"Your hands are shaking." He kissed her neck once more, then backed away, holding the frosted cinnamon roll like the prize it was.

He was getting inside her head and she could barely stand it in there herself right now. She wished for clarity. How to move forward?

Hold me and never let me go!

"I'm not ready," she said, her hands trembling again. "We still don't seem to understand each other's methods of communication. I get it, you're not a big talker, but I'm..." With a bewildered expression, she moved away from him and said, "I need you to stop kissing me."

"Kat, don't shut me out. I'm telling you that you need my strength, my attention. You think you're so tough, but you don't have to do everything alone. Ask for help, for crissakes!"

"There's a lot of stuff in play right now and I feel like a dirt dobber is building a nest in my head." She worked her way methodically through the pile of rolls, spreading the frosting as she talked, trying to remain unemotional when her words made her want to howl.

"Until we know if I can carry this baby..."

She hated herself for bringing up the topic that would make

him shutter himself from his emotions. She might as well get it all out there.

"We haven't discussed what we want out of life after," Kat said with a sigh. "Right now, all I know is I'm trying to provide a stable environment to raise Lilly in. Wonderful, you are. Stable, you're not. And I know you feel like I tricked you into this pregnancy. It's not much of a start."

His voice vibrated with emotion. "You talk too much, Kat. You never know when to quit."

She thought he was going to kiss her, passion and anger warring in his eyes, but he took a huge bite of his cinnamon roll and chewed the thing like it was rawhide.

He swallowed. "Enough fooling around for me this morning. I've got a little work to do while you get Lilly off to school. I reckon I'll head into the store after a bit. I can drop these for you at the Mill. I need to talk to Lana and meet Garrett, anyway."

"You're pretty sure of yourself," Kat said, and he gave her a cocky grin.

"Make me a chore list of the heavy lifting you need me to pick up for you, and I mean it. If I find you're overextending yourself, I'll be on you like a hen on a June bug. I can see you don't want to stand still for that."

He fidgeted with his hat, gave his hard won treat a scowl. "Meet me for lunch. I'll have Mom make up some sandwiches and you can give me a hand with my inventory lists."

He took another bite and threw the rest of his cinnamon roll on the counter. He left the kitchen, apparently uninterested in her response.

Kat tracked his retreat with narrowed eyes. He was spoiling for a fight, telling her how it was going to be. She debated chasing after him to hit him in the head with the rest of his roll, or blowing him off so she could watch him make a mess of everything with his big talk.

It would serve him right. She opted for the latter and silently frosted the rest of the rolls while her temper seethed. Who did he think he was?

This was her ranch, and she had tractors to handle the heavy lifting. She fed square bales to her own few horses, but last year she'd had to have round bales hauled in for the rescue animals. There were too many. She'd just feed all the horses rounds this winter. She had a good used tractor with a hay spike she could operate just fine. The grain, well... she'd use coffee cans instead of five-gallon buckets, no big.

All winter. She was going to be helpless until next spring. That was daunting. What if there was another ice storm?

At least Eli had been working that back fence, so there would be more grazing land next spring. He seemed to be making progress, anyway. She'd noticed the materials disappearing. She needed to remember to get more fencing steeples next time she went to the store.

It ticked her off that she couldn't fix her own fence. It was a matter of pride. Jake had put the kibosh on her riding almost immediately, though, and so much of the back fence Eli was working was too rocky and hilly to drive a truck. One good thing, if Jake got his store open, she wouldn't have to drive so far for supplies.

Ugh. She'd make that demanding man a list of a few things she'd need his help with, but very few. He could just go play storekeeper and leave her alone to run her ranch her own way. He never failed to get her dander up.

In was nice to know she wasn't alone, but she'd be hogtied before she'd take orders. There was work to do that she could do just fine. In a few hours, a gracious lady was coming to adopt two mares, and Kat wanted them both looking sharp.

Any adopters that made it to this stage of her vetting process had worked for it. These critters had suffered too much already if they were on her ranch, and trust was hard for some of them.

She worked tirelessly to prepare the horses for adoption and hoped they would find families who would love them always. This woman's decision to home two of her rescues gave her renewed hope that more of them would find homes, too.

She boxed the cinnamon rolls and set them out for Jake to deliver. That would give her a little more time today. All these thoughts of winter reminded her she better get busy. She headed out to the barn to get started on the day's chores. Maybe she should ask Santa to find her a work brickle cowboy for Christmas.

Jake made some phone calls and arranged a few heavy equipment salesmen to visit him next week, then hedged his bets, making a commitment for weekly grain deliveries to fill his silos. The western wear was tougher. He'd have to get Kat's help there.

Time to go face his possibly ticked-off wife. She rarely cottoned to taking orders, and he'd been pretty specific. But man, you could plant that woman and grow ten acres of stubborn. She was a firecracker, that was for sure. He found her feeding hay to her horses in their stalls.

"I said to leave that to me."

"Well, Mr. Merchant, this wasn't one of the things on my list," she said. Too sweetly. "I broke the bales into thirds, so I'm well under my weight limit, boss."

He glared at the hay in her hand. "You're a real glutton for punishment, aren't ya?"

Jake studied Kat's complexion and worried. She was too pale. He rubbed at the stubble on his chin.

Shaving is such a hassle.

He had given a brief thought to cleaning up, but his jeans weren't filthy yet and he had a ton more grunt work to do, so he'd settled for a clean shirt. He could change it again before going into the store.

"I'll help, then you'll be done faster." He wondered how best to tackle what was on his mind. Apparently, he picked the wrong tactic, as usual.

"You look terrible, Kat. Go take a nap before you come in. We have to discuss how we're going to break up the duties so you get a suitable amount of rest and then I'll need to know how to take over in a few months when you go full-time bedrest."

"You... need to check your highhandedness, hon. You're not going to tell me how to run my life or my business. I didn't ask for your help."

She glared at him with narrowed dark eyes, and he realized he was dangerously close to being cussed out. He lowered his voice so perhaps they could skip the shouting match. She needed to stay calm.

"Listen, love, you didn't ask for my help, but you need it. If we're going to bring this baby out, adopt Lilly, and keep your horses fed, we're going to have to work together."

He wondered if there was a chance on earth of her being able to carry the baby full term. It was terrifying to think about being responsible for a little one, but it was growing on him. If only he wasn't fearful for Kat's life.

"Jake—"

He held up his hand. "Understand I'm worried about you because you're so fearless, and..."

He was going to say irrational, but possibly not a good idea. If he could fix their marriage, honesty was going to be key, but maybe not quite that honest.

"I know it's early yet, but you agreed to limit yourself to light duty work. I'm going to hold you to it."

"This is daily chores, Jake! I'm not just going to lie down and die."

The words hit him, and he knew it showed on his face. That was exactly what he was afraid of. His voice held the anguish he felt. "The chances of you carrying a child are slim to none. I know you can't bear the loss again, love, and neither can I. You have to be careful."

Kat sighed. "You win."

She took off her gloves and put them in her back pocket, then reached out to take his hand. The gesture was meant to share the pain of their loss, something they should have managed before instead of waiting so long.

He tugged her into a hug and she stiffened before squeezing him tight, so tight he could feel the pressure of her abdomen against his own. He was grateful for the contact—and the hope.

She pulled away and swiped at a tear forming in her eye.

"So, if you're going to run my money makers by the Mill,

you better get cracking. At this rate, you'll be delivering those rolls directly to the Red Hat Club ladies themselves, and they might not let a handsome young stud like yourself leave after they see what you've brought them. Tell Lana I'll stop in later and make sure you survived the experience."

"Sure thing." He grinned but tenderly pushed the stray hairs from her cheek, wishing he could hold her until the hurt went away.

That doesn't work and you know it.

The pain went deeper than that.

"How about I rest a little after I get my two mares off, then I'll meet you at the store? Why don't you load the rolls into my truck and I'll drive the farm truck?" He nodded, and she handed him her keys. "This afternoon we can discuss our partnerships, both of them. Thanks for looking out for me."

"Sure kiddo, me and you. It's always been us."

Tenderness filled his tone, and Kat melted. "Now it's me and Lilly and this baby and you. I'm not sure where we stand, Jake, but we can try to figure it out."

If only she could trust him with all her burdens, her uncertainty about the future and the pain of the past. She would let him help her with the physical stuff, but she had to manage her feelings by herself. When he was tired of this game, she'd need the reserve strength just to move on.

"So how about you let me finish the hay, then I'll make the delivery? You don't need any help with that?" He nodded at a truck and trailer pulling into her drive.

"No worries. Just don't be late or Lana will hang me. I would've taken them early if you hadn't offered."

He nodded and grabbed up an armload of hay, and she turned to meet the lady who would give two very special mares their forever homes.

On her way into town proper, Kat swung by the Mill to see that Jake actually delivered. He was notorious for setting off to do something with the best intentions and getting sidetracked by some fascinating aspect of *something*.

Lana greeted Kat warmly, and her face glowed with the contentment of an expectant mother.

"Look at you, Kat," Lana said. "After all your tough talk, I see Jake has blindsided you again with what can only be called his charm. He was quite a hit with the Widow Donovan's group. I thought his eyes were going to bug out when he got a load of their outrageous hats and blouses, but he was the perfect gentleman."

As she pouted, Lana tapped her foot impatiently on the ground with a hand on her hip. "He gave each of those little gals one of your cinnamon rolls and didn't save me one."

"He ate yours." Kat smiled and gave her best friend a gentle side hug. Pregnancy was so beautiful on her. "So, he made it and survived, then?"

"Oh yeah, he gushed about how they should all visit the western wear section as soon as he got his store open. Promised to stock them red cowboy hats. Our Jake, a store owner."

She pushed a wild hair that had escaped her braid back into place and tilted her head quizzically at Kat. "Are you okay? You look a little peaked. Do you want to sit down?" She gestured at a table in the small bar outside the dining room, where she had been sitting and visiting with Tabby.

Kat felt a sardonic laugh escape. So Jake had left it up to her. And his mom was here. Great.

"No, I'm meeting Jake. I just wanted to confirm that you wanted an extra dozen rolls for your group next week and... mostly, I thought I should let you know I'm pregnant."

Lana's reaction was the uncomfortable look Kat expected. Lana visited them on the road after they lost the baby and she'd seen what the couple had gone through, the way they treated each other. Jaime had come, too, and the girls united for Kat, all coddling her, but it hadn't helped.

"Does Jake know?" Lana asked. "I mean, I guess it's his?" She glanced at Tabby with a grin, then smacked Kat in the arm. "I told you if you were serious about a divorce, mail him the papers. I knew you two wouldn't be able to keep your hands off each other."

Tabby interrupted. "What are you guys going to do?"

"Don't worry, Mom," Kat said with a sigh. "Jake and I are grown-ups and we can figure this out."

Kat saw a challenge in Tabby's eyes that made her blood heat. She frowned at her mother-in-law.

"Are you, now?" Tabby spun around, pacing the length of the room, and tracked back to where Kat was standing. "So you guys aren't getting a divorce?"

Kat didn't answer, not ready to go into her uncertain feelings with Tabby while Lana just sat quietly. She was talking to the wrong friend.

"Kat, you're making me forget how happy you made me when you told me you were adopting Lilly. The idea of being a grandmother after all this time..."

"But..."

Tabby shushed her, and she shut up to avoid arguing. Her mother-in-law's heart was in the right place. Tabby blamed herself for her children's unhappy childhoods, as they were constantly uprooted and exposed to the chaos of military bases and rodeo scenes. Kat knew Tabby also blamed Lug.

"I've never met two more selfish people," Tabby said. "You better think about what kind of life that baby is going to have if you two can't get your act together. And what about how you've dragged Lilly into this mess you call a marriage?"

"Look, I'm not saying it's a lost cause anymore, I just don't know..." Kat tried to interrupt, but Tabby wasn't done.

"My own family struggled through tough times and I wanted better for my children. Jake knows how I feel. I guess he's fine with whatever you decide, like always. Doubtless y'all aren't even listening to each other. I knew seeing him with those cinnamon rolls was a bad omen."

Lana was just nodding along.

"Are you done, yet, oh loving mother-in-law of mine?"

Kat was exasperated with her reaction, but it was no less than she expected. If she could just get away—but all she had to look forward to was this stubborn woman's son.

If only she didn't love hard luck cases so much, she wouldn't have made the twins her special project that summer long ago.

"Almost." Tabby gave Kat a quick hug. "I love you. Jake left mad. I may have gotten in his face, too. But you kids..." She just shook her head. "You're like my own, Kat, so I feel like you'll know it comes from a place of love when I tell you two to get it together."

As soon as Kat saw the determined expression in Tabby's eyes, she knew things had gone south. Jake's mom had gotten involved in their business, and her best friend had sold her out.

Chapter 8

Kat found herself back at a lovely table at Falls Mill a few hours later. She and Jake had finished taking notes for a preliminary inventory and had groused at each other's ideas several times. It'd been a rough day, and wasn't looking up.

Jake gave her a sheepish look over his menu. "Sorry I didn't ask Mom to make sandwiches. She was in such a bad mood that I don't think she would have given me a slice of bread if I asked. It was a piece of her mind she was offering."

"Yep, she was tough today," Kat mumbled. She hadn't been in the mood to eat, but Jake insisted.

"Medium well, plain, no bun? Grilled onions on the side?" Jake gave her a questioning look, and she responded with a nod.

He ordered their burgers from the young waitress, who Kat knew would be their cook and cashier, too. Kobi was the Rock Star of Lana's employees.

"Also a plain baked potato and a tall unsweet tea," Kat said, passing back the menu she hadn't needed. "Thanks, Kobi, we appreciate you."

When they were alone sipping their tea, Kat made a conscious decision to try a conversation instead of a shouting match. She could feel his temper brewing, so she attempted to be courteous.

Despite their experiences living on the road, she'd noticed they'd forgotten the importance of fighting quietly. Kat had grown accustomed to a peaceful routine since parting ways with her husband, and arguing was the last thing on her mind—until he returned home.

"Your mom said you were a real hit with the ladies and focused on drumming up business for the store," Kat said. "Good call. I'm surprised you got away from them, though, after that stunt with Vivian the other day."

"Yeah, I knew I needed a plan," Jake agreed. "I told them we'd start stocking red cowgirl hats. The ladies were all wearing purple shirts, too. I don't know what it's all about, but how about we try some purple cowboy boots, too, see if the old gals will bite?"

Jake had added about ten packets of sugar to his tea, and tasted it to see if he had it sweet enough. Apparently, it passed, because he drank half the glass before going on.

"They looked like a pretty wild bunch of white-haired ladies. I recognized several of them, but I wouldn't have figured them to wear such get-ups."

Kat nodded. "They are... memorable. Sounds like you've got it all figured out."

"Not quite, especially mom, but she'll come around," Jake said. "Speaking of costumes, are you sure about hosting a Halloween party? Do you think you should stress the baby out? Let's figure a way out for me to oversee it."

Kat noticed the concern etched on his face and softened her growl, but she narrowed her eyes at him.

"I think I can handle a simple party for Lilly. I'll keep it modest." Taking a napkin from the antique holder in the center of the table, she began to shred it into small pieces, laying the white strips along the white lines in the green-checked tablecloth.

"I'm curious," she continued. "You've been here a week now, and I admit, I'm surprised at how well you're settling in. I noticed, though, that you make big plans without asking me, and I guess I haven't been direct with you either..."

She could tell he was getting irritated because his eyes went dark. "That's an understatement."

"Wait." She held out her hand, halting the canned responses, then slid her hand over her napkin strips, wadding them up in a ball that she spun in her fingers while she watched him. "We have to talk about the baby, about Lilly, about us. Where do we go from here?"

He seemed to consider her instead of popping off the hot-headed response on the tip of his tongue.

"I find myself wishing things could go back to the way they were, Kat. I miss the time we spent together on the road and the freedom it brought us. But more than anything, I wish for the baby to be born and for me to be part of the life you're making here with Lilly and Eli."

He reached out and took the shredded napkin from her, catching her hand in his.

"If you asked me if I wanted to be a dad two weeks ago, I would have said no. Knowing a part of me is growing in you is heady. I don't know if I can make a living here or not. All I know is the road. But I'm going to work my tail off to make it happen. I want the 'us' part."

She pulled back gently. "I wish I could trust you'd always feel that way."

"We were happy once, Kat. What happened?"

He looked forlorn, and it hurt. She appeared to have a knack for hurting him, so it seemed fitting that she should suffer, too.

"What happened was we stopped talking to one another."

"We talk all the time." He rubbed his head and looked longingly at the ball cap on the seat beside him. "We just don't talk about the feelings junk all the time."

His protest was sincere, and Kat wondered how much of this was her fault. "We talk at each other, or around each other. We talked about the rodeo, but whenever I wanted you to consider an alternate lifestyle," she paused, "such as the ranch I work so hard for, you never wanted to hear it. Telling myself I was happy and everything was okay wasn't working for me anymore. I had to make a change."

"Divorce?" His blue eyes were deep swirls of emotion. "I thought it would be me and you forever. Why do you always have to be so dramatic about everything?"

"This sounds like an old argument." Kat sighed. "So I'm dramatic. You used to like that about me."

"Before you decided what we had wasn't good enough for the princess of Riverbend Falls. You've been holding it against me. I have a tough time being in the same town as my folks, which is why I didn't come back. Didn't wanna end up like them, but looks like I messed up again. I just don't enjoy having to see it so close. They fight like beasts and throw me and Jaime around like bones to pick at each other with."

"Baloney. You keep your folks in check better than anyone. Jake, you didn't want to give up the feeling of being adored by a group of girls in tight shorts and Stetsons who made up your fan club. You're not fooling me. Same old story, work first, feelings later. You're about you."

Her anger was boiling inside her, and she felt like she could explode. They both dredged up the past like it was a sunken ship, impossible to salvage.

"Foods here." Their waitress looked nervous, and Kat realized the few other diners were looking at them interestedly. It seemed they would be the talk of the town once again.

"Thanks, Kobi," Kat said. "Sorry about the noise. Perhaps now we'll eat instead of talk."

She gave Jake a pointed glare and bit into her hamburger patty. This living amongst neighbors just got more challenging. She ate her food silently, yet her mind was racing with thoughts she couldn't ignore.

"Maybe we can figure out how to work together again. Not me doing my thing and you doing yours, but... I still can't believe you just bought the Hitchin' Post. I wish you would've asked me before you did something so big."

Jake jumped in without testing the water. It was always like this with him. He was so impulsive. A huge list of descriptors came to mind—selfish, childish, inconsiderate...

"Like adopting a child? Be careful where you cast stones,

darlin.”

Kat could tell by the stubborn set of his jaw that he wasn't going to make things easy, but she was determined to find a solution that would satisfy most everyone. She'd long ago come to terms with the fact that Jake was not emotionally available to her.

"I can see it in your eyes. Want me to say the words for you? Selfish, childish, inconsiderate? Am I close? What about you, honey? You were planning to divorce me and keep my family a secret from me. That's a pretty big chunk of selfish in the making."

"But I didn't tell you about Lilly because it happened after I saw you. And I didn't know about the baby!" She felt near tears at how everything was twisting on her. "Besides, how could I get custody with you around? You're a child yourself, unable to commit to any action beyond your next thrill. Seems to me you wouldn't want to be around."

"So you keep saying. Let me get this straight. When I came to town last week, you were eagerly awaiting the chance to tell me we were adopting a child together? Because that's not how it looked from where I was. Seemed to me you were hiding her."

His icy glare made Kat prickly. He was riled, and if she said a word, he was likely to yell at her.

"Despite the promises we made, it seems like you've already given up," Jake grumbled, clearly frustrated. "You left divorce papers on my pillow and didn't even have the courage to tell me about them..."

He crumbled his napkin and threw it at his half-eaten burger, pushing it away. "You hurt me, Kat. I loved you that night with the passion of a man who'd been given a second chance. I laid awake that night thinking I could make it up to you, the fact we'd lost our friendship along the way. Then in the morning, bam, the heartless woman split the scene. Just me and my thoughts again."

Kat felt the tears threatening to flood over and tried to get them under control before she lost every scrap of pride in this booth. He was right, of course. She was the selfish one.

"I'm not going to rehash the past with you—"

"It's not the past, Kat. This is our life right now. You're working diligently to keep me shut out and I'll be perfectly honest with you. It's working." He looked away. "If you shut me out, I still want to be my baby's father, and we could do partial custody..."

"It's my baby," she whispered.

"No, Kat. When you started a family, it was blessed with two parents." He stood up and threw two twenties down on the table to cover the tab and tip.

"Not the brightest parents, but all the same. Make your plans with that in mind. It doesn't matter if you're through with me. I'll be in your life for the next nineteen years if we both live that long, and I'm gonna be right up in your ring for the next seven months. Deal with it."

He walked out, leaving Kat to scramble after him. The moment the door chimed behind her, she knew the town would buzz with the revelation Kat and Jake were pregnant—and still fighting.

She'd cried herself to sleep again. Jake was going to get what he wanted, and she'd end up as an afterthought. His own business, the town would love him, Lilly adored him, her baby... She couldn't stop him, even if she wanted to.

If only she could say things better. If only she wasn't such a coward, then they could have talked things over before things had to escalate to threats.

If only she would just tell him she loved him and she was sorry.

There were compromises to be made. They could be a family, no matter where they were. Trust was what this was about, and Kat felt like a dog because she couldn't give him a chance.

Jake arrived in the kitchen promptly at five.

"About this Halloween party..."

"Don't start on me so early," Kat moaned, scratching her nose, wishing he'd go back to sleeping in.

"I want to help," Jake said. "I've been thinking hard and you gotta hear me out. If we have the party at the Hitchin' Post, we can make it the grand opening, and use the legend about the old barn being haunted to punch things up a bit."

She could practically feel the excitement emanating from him as he looked at her, hoping for a truce.

"I can't believe you remembered about the ghost." Due to the lack of a 'sighting' in her lifetime, Kat had forgotten about the old tales. "I bet that will bring out the curiosity seekers."

"It always interested me as a kid. Whenever someone mentioned the barn to me, the first thing that came to mind was the ghost story. The kids even called Hank a haunt behind his back for a while. I put a stop to that."

He mock punched his hand and Kat snorted. "You did not!"

Kat remembered the days when she thought her husband was the center of the universe, and his warm smile made her feel like she was the luckiest woman alive. He had that smile now.

"Anyway, I've been looking at the way other places capitalize on their ghost stories, and we can do that here. Pull in more tourists."

"It sounds... incredible." It also seemed far-fetched he wasn't still mad, but if he was willing to let the sleeping dog lie, that suited her.

"If we get Falls Mill to sponsor a chili cook off at the park, we could use hay rides to bring folks up to Main Street from the water and back. That'd make it easy for visitors to see how close and handy our town is."

She nodded, and he took it as agreement. Didn't sound like a bad idea.

"I can do all the heavy work. You get a party for Lilly, and I get a bunch of people in my store all at once. We'll invite the other stores. See how it all plays out?"

"We?" She raised an eyebrow at him.

"If it's what you want, I'll leave you in peace as soon as you're back on your feet, but I wasn't kidding about you spending your last trimester on your back so we might as well work together and enjoy it for now. I'll sign the papers then if you'll make sure my custodial rights are intact."

Ouch. There it was. He didn't see the look in her eyes, but Kat knew his sentence was harsh because she'd hurt him. And forgiveness didn't come easy to Jake.

I love you and I'm sorry.

Try as she might, she couldn't will the words from her lips, but they were on the tip of her tongue.

As the next two weeks flew by, she felt like she was moving to the beat of a complicated song. Moments of perfect harmony always seemed on the verge of being disrupted by a sense of calamity. The dread built between them as Kat continued to avoid Jake emotionally and depend on him physically.

She still hadn't mentioned her dizzy spells, but with Jake watching everything she ate, she was gaining weight, and the dizzy spells came less often. She was able to convince herself it was no big deal until she saw the doctor again.

"I can tell you I'm concerned, Kat. If you can't keep your insulin stabilized, the risk of miscarriage goes from moderate to high. I'm going to want you to keep daily journals. Monitor your insulin levels more closely for me, okay? You're already one of my best patients. You keep in shape, eat right, but..."

The elderly doctor rubbed his hand over the bridge of his nose in a sign Kat recognized as frustration. Her heart hammered as he continued, "I'm worried about there being an irregular heartbeat."

"What do you mean? That isn't supposed to be something I have to worry about. Proper diet and rest, that's what you said. Honest, I've been careful."

She could hear herself becoming hysterical and wished for the tenth time Jake had been around this morning. He was supposed to meet her, but she hadn't told him why. She was going to surprise him, and ask him to come with to her checkup. He had a knack for calming her, helping her see the bright side.

At least he'd left a note. "Out of pocket, back by dinner."

She should have expected it, but the letdown still stung.

Doc Robbins shook his head. "You seem in good health, but we're only at fifteen weeks."

He gave her a warning look, reminding her of many lectures she'd received about the dangers of pregnancy and diabetes. Now was the time to bring up the fainting spells, but he was scowling at her.

"So, the baby is okay?" she asked, touching the belly holding her precious cargo.

He stepped back. "I'm concerned about the effort your body will have to put forth to support the growth of both babies."

The blood rushed to her head, and she woke a second later with the doc standing over her. Thank God she'd been sitting on his exam table or she'd have smacked her head when she fainted.

"Have you been having fainting spells?" There was naked concern on his face.

"Twins?"

She breathed the word, caught in a place between terror and wonder. She'd dreamed of twins once when she was young and foolish. When she believed nothing could damage the love she and Jake shared... now the dream seemed hazy. Good gravy, two babies!

"You look pale. Lie there a minute, I'll be back."

Doc came back seconds later with an orange juice box and instructed her to sip slowly. He shoved his hands in his pockets and turned toward her chart, his voice more uncertain than she'd ever heard it. He was a bossy doc.

"I want this to work for you, but... I've known you since you came to this town and I knew your adopted parents well. They would be proud to see what a beautiful and spirited young woman you've grown into, and the beautiful thing you're doing for little Lilly." He shook his head. "I'll want to monitor you closely in hopes... well, we'll take extra precautions."

Kat couldn't talk yet, feeling like a little girl as she listened, sipping her juice box.

"You know I'm not one to put stock in gossip, but they say Jake's re-opening the Hitchin' Post. Is he helping you through this? He doesn't have a strong record for seeing things through, but maybe... I worry about you, Kat. I know..."

"I'm never alone, Doc. I have Eli and Lilly, the horses... Jake and I are adults and—"

"Young lady—"

"Please, Doc. Thank you for your concern. I know you mean well, but affairs of the heart are out of this decision. We have two little lives to help into this world."

She touched her tummy, her eyes misting, and the doc smiled, his furrowed brow relaxing.

"Good enough then. Start keeping a list of your food and drink intake for me, and if you have any more fainting spells, make a note of the details for me." He wrote a date on an appointment card and handed it to her. "I'd like to see Jake next time. There are certain sexual precautions we need to discuss, as well as..."

"Doc Robbins!"

"Sex is perfectly healthy, but in your particular condition, I'd prefer to discuss safe sex with both of you."

Kat rolled her eyes. "Doctor Robbins, if you dare mention sex to Jake, in or out of my presence, I'll make sure Fran knows why you aren't able to lose those extra pounds despite the diet she's had you on for months. Falls Mill cinnamon rolls ring a bell?"

He grimaced at her. "You play hardball, young lady. Mum's the word. Now get out of here, but monitor yourself, Kat. I'll worry until I've safely delivered those babes."

She stood. "Thanks, Doc. Me too. I'll ask Jake next time," she said, shaking the card thoughtfully. "Twins." She grinned at him, suddenly excited. "Thanks!"

She hugged him and headed out in a daze.

Chapter 9

"Absolutely not." Lana shook her head, her tidy blonde braid swinging crazily. "Vivian told me about it last week and I've been avoiding her and Ralph just so I don't get caught in the dragnet."

"Please. Just give me some idea about how to play the council. Vivian's got everyone worked up about trying to renew their businesses. I'm not into all this decision making, and people keep asking me questions I can't even begin to answer."

Lana looked at her sympathetically and Kat stuck out her bottom lip, batting her eyelashes at her friend. She held out a bribe of cinnamon rolls, which Lana promptly snagged and tucked into the top of her handbag.

Kat knew she'd be able to catch Lana this morning and hoped to avoid Jamie, sort of. The thought of telling her sister-in-law she was pregnant with twins made her pause, not wanting to witness the storm of feelings in Jaime's vivid turquoise eyes. Not wanting to deal with it.

"I can't believe this has blown up like it has. Everyone's talking about Jake like he's some kind of hero come home instead of... y'know." Kat felt her face heat in a sudden flush.

Jake and Jaime were ornery from the get go when they moved to town, but it was what made them so fun—constantly playing pranks around town and sneaking around to not get caught.

Jaime's worldliness awed and fascinated Kat, and their friendship quickly blossomed. Jake had a thing for Kat, and things got a little messy, but they eventually figured it out.

The love-fueled spats of the early days were just the beginning of their ongoing tiffs. The memory of the hurtful words they exchanged a few years ago still lingered, straining the affection between her and Jamie. She intended to remedy it. Just not today.

"So how are things going with you and Mr. Wonderful?"

"Hah! He's making me crazy. Anyway, that's sort of why I'm here. I think Tabby is going to help him at the store, so I still have time to do my own work, but this restoration deal is killing me. We need help. I throw myself at your mercy."

"Sorry. Way too busy." Lana grinned and rubbed her tummy, then bumped Kat with her hip, a familiar gesture. "What made him suggest such a thing, anyway? He had to figure charging in with big changes in mind would ruffle feathers. You'd think he'd want to keep a low profile."

"I don't know," Kat moaned. "I guess I'm going to have to help him. Mrs. Bunsen, bless her aging heart, keeps asking me if she's going to need new awnings."

She looked at Lana and groaned... serious whining.

"Cynthia's been looking at me like I'm some kind of earwig, like I said her store needed work. Sheriff Tate's asking me about putting trash cans on the sidewalks. It's like I'm supposed to solve the tourism problem... with weird details. It's weighing on my mind."

The girls were sitting on the bench outside the Falls Mill restaurant on the deck overlooking the river. The fall trees towered over Kat, bursting with vibrant color, yet despite their beauty, they seemed to be weighed down by a sense of sadness, as if they knew the long, cold winter was coming.

She knew how they felt.

"Rumors are circulating that Jake plans to revive tourism and put Riverbend Falls back on the map. He's re-opening the feed store, for heaven's sake. Great for my gas budget, but how is that going to drag in tourists? You know I'm good at getting people to do things, but I don't have a game plan here. This is messing with my rhythms. Everything is messing with me."

Lana was hiding her smile, but not very well. "So, he's got ya riled, huh? Is the rumor true that you are..."

"Yup, twins. Jake's treating me like I'm made of glass and it's driving me nuts. Lilly has even started asking him for things that I used to help with. You know how he feels about riding? He's been teaching Lilly. Not by example, of course. The only saddle time she gets is if Eli takes her, since riding is another forbidden pleasure for me. Would you believe he won't let me... ugh—I hate being bossed around."

Kat hung her head. Her closest friend was liable to call her out about her green-eyed monster, and she didn't want to face it. "All that stuff aside, how much is it going to cost? If you won't do it out of the good grace of your heart—"

"That's your shtick, shweetheart. I'm all about the cash." Lana patted her pocket. "Fifty bucks an hour to do the organizing, but you and Jake manage it from there. No one gets to know I had anything to do with this because then they'll recruit me. I've got my hands full..." She rubbed her pregnant tummy again.

"I'm sorry. That wasn't very thoughtful of me."

"No, it's okay. I've actually never felt better. I just don't want Garrett riding me like Jake is going to ride you." She patted Kat's hand sympathetically.

"Look, you do your thing and get people fired up to believe whatever you're going to tell them. I'll put together a few vague options for Jake to suggest to the council, and most likely, nothing will change. That should get him out of hot water for opening his big mouth." Lana laughed, and it reminded Kat of old times, when they'd practically been a posse. "Everyone will probably forget the whole thing. If not, our little town will look a little prettier. Stop worrying, if it works, it helps my business, too, so win-win."

Kat grinned, shaking her ponytail in relief. Lana married earlier this year and Falls Mill had been born where the ghosts of Lana's past lay. The transformation of the old Mill and campground had saved the land, and her best friend.

Lana's baby was due in November, but she was still healthy and mobile as a young colt. She'd had a delicate first semester, but had grown more resilient as the baby inside her grew. Kat would have no such luck.

The girls stood, and Kat gave Lana a brief but powerful hug.

"Congratulations, right? On the twin's thing. Are you scared?"

Kat breathed a deep sigh. "Terrified. I'm being careful, and it's still incredibly early. The closer I get to the six-month mark, the more dangerous it will be. Jake probably won't let me out of bed for the last three months."

"He hasn't lost his fire, has he? You two were made for each other."

"Hmph." Kat grumbled. "He's wilder than a turpentined cat. He's patient with Lilly, though. I love him for that."

"Well, just be careful, Kat."

Her meaning was twofold, and Kat knew it. She needed to be careful not to hurt anyone or get hurt herself.

"Cool. I'm out of here. I'm supposed to meet Jake at the store and I want to duck everyone else for a bit—too late." Kat saw Vivian round the corner, and she knew she was had.

"Karita, dear. I've been hoping to run into you, and I heard you were here. There've been a pile of inquiries about your project and…"

"I was just working on some fine points for Jake, Vivian dear. If you'd like, I can send him over this afternoon to collect your questions. I think he might be ready to present something tomorrow evening at the council meeting."

Vivian's eyes were shining with something unholy and Kat felt a little guilty, but Jake had brought this on himself.

"Good. Send him by my office about three and I'll have a list for him." She tapped a perfectly manicured fingernail against perfectly painted lips. "Yep, this is certainly livening up the town. Lana, dear, can you stop by the office later?"

"Sure, Viv." They watched the feisty sixty-year-old sashay away, and Lana turned to Kat with a resigned sigh. "Snared. I knew she'd find some way to drag me into this. She made a special trip, too. Paperwork only, I won't get dragged into the politics."

"You're the best. I'll tell Jake to look for your bill." Kat grinned. "See ya, Lan."

She ambled toward her truck parked near the Mills little store. Now she just had to... a lightheaded feeling hit her just as she reached her door handle.

Terrified of falling down in the parking lot where anyone could see, she held on tight as the feeling passed. The worry didn't pass so quickly. She slid gently onto the bench seat and methodically fired up the engine, waiting a moment before shifting it into gear.

She'd be in big trouble if she passed out behind the wheel.

Six years before, when she lost Melody, she had blacked out, falling to the floor, and woke up empty. Her baby removed— her heart so bruised she'd wished for death to take the pain away.

But she'd been at six months then. She was barely showing now at fifteen weeks. It would not happen this time. She would be careful—she'd lean on Jake.

She was supposed to be at the feed store by now. They were expecting a load of tractors from the dealer in Crestview, and she knew Jake was writing a check so big it hurt. He was investing a lot into making Hank's his own.

Kat was going to come around. She didn't know why she couldn't stop doubting her husband, but she was determined to push away the question bothering her.

How long would it last?

He was in the exciting phase now, buying and spending, but once it became business as usual, what would happen?

Driving past the Inn and Out, she thought of Jake's folks. She wondered if the two would ever get over their differences. They didn't exactly inspire hope in her situation.

Tabby blamed Lug for her kids leaving town, but Kat knew the twins never felt like they belonged. For certain she'd thought Jaime would never come back, and she'd been dead wrong.

Jaime was freshly married herself, and living up the way a piece with Tad Stone, helping raise his two sons. Despite her inability to quit being mad at her old friend, she was desperately proud of Jaime. Kat found herself hopeful both twins would realize they were home.

In front of the Inn, a sleek sports car parked, and a cute blonde got out of the passenger seat. She looked vaguely familiar, but Kat didn't dwell on it as she drove past and parked in front of the feed store.

She walked around the outside of the store, drawn by the sound of laughter and the unmistakable clanking of machinery coming from the back where the "haunted" barn stood. Kat couldn't decide if the scene before her was alarming or delightful.

Lilly drove one of the new orange tractors with ease as Jake sat beside her. He was enjoying the sight of all the brand-new tractors, combines, and hay equipment on display in the back parking area of *his* store.

The tractor's engine purred to a stop as, with just a little coaching, Lilly put it in park and turned off the key. He lifted her down from the seat. She ran across the parking lot toward Kat with her eyes shining, but Jake hung back.

The school had called and said Lilly was sick. Eli had been busy with a sick horse and Kat had been out with Lana, so Jake had gone and picked her up. Lilly confided in him she wasn't sick. She was upset because some kids at school were picking on her, telling her Kat wouldn't want somebody else's kid when she was going to have her own.

He'd assured her Kat was capable of more love than the universe was big. Her big heart never emptied and anyway, Lilly was Kat's daughter now. She seemed mollified, but she'd asked him not to tell Kat, and that worried him.

Secrets were never good, and he could see the skepticism in Lilly's eyes. He guessed he'd let it play out, see how things went.

"Why aren't you in school, honey? Are you sick?" Kat asked.

Jake's heart melted as he watched Kat embrace Lilly. As any

mother would, she knelt and checked her daughter's forehead for a temperature, her expression filled with concern.

"I played hooky because this baby school is stupid. Anyway, I'm glad I did. I got to drive a tractor. It's hard, too. You have to know what all the little letters mean, and then the levers work all kinds of different stuff. I moved the bucket up and down!"

Lilly pulled on her ponytail and Jake wondered if it was a conscious move to imitate Kat when she was nervous, or just a fluke the girls had the same tic. Either way, it was cute.

He met Kat's inquisitive gaze. "So, me and this young lady had a tough talk about how she avoided her responsibility by pretending to be sick and she said she'd pitch in with cooking and washing dishes tonight as a punishment, right?"

He thought she was going to whine again, like she had when they'd first discussed it, but to her credit, she said, "Yes, sir. I don't like doing dishes, so I won't pretend I'm sick when I'm not. Sorry, Mom."

Kat looked shocked, and he was proud of himself. He'd done a real fatherly thing, dishing out punishment and all.

"Well, ladies, what do you say we go to the house now and we'll fool around down by the river until time for Lilly and I to cook?"

Kat stood and rested her hand on Lilly's shoulder. He noticed her mood shift, and he wondered if he'd made a mistake. Even though she tried to hide it, her face showed she was mad at him... again.

"Sorry, Jake. You have an appointment with Vivian at three to discuss your proposal for the meeting tomorrow night. Lana is working on some sort of speech for you to make so everyone will get off my..."

She glanced down at Lilly and moderated the irritation out of her voice. He was grateful to the kid for the silent reinforcement against Kat's ire. She went on more calmly.

"You're paying fifty bucks an hour for Lana, so I'd be careful about wasting her time. I'll consent to the punishment you two agreed on, but we won't be going to fool around down at the water. Lilly can start on her chores, then clean her room until it's time to help *whoever's* cooking."

"Kat, I..." he tried.

"If you get home in time, I suppose I could let you lift the heavy dishes for me so I don't hurt myself."

Kat's sharp tone caught Lilly off guard, but the tender look she received when she took Kat's hand reassured her.

"I'm sorry honey, I didn't mean to get loud. My emotions are just a little funny feeling right now."

"Mine, too."

Lilly mumbled it quietly, but Jake was listening. He doubted Kat heard. She was so busy glaring at him he doubted she was thinking about anything but the source of her anger.

Jake wondered who she was apologizing to, then felt like a fool for wishing it could be him. Kat was lovely to everyone in the world except him. And what did it say about his own sanity that no other woman would ever suit him the way she did?

Love could make you suffer for real.

He gave a slight bow, leaving it to Kat's imagination to wonder if he was mocking Riverbend Falls's princess or not.

"It seems, fair maidens, it tis my duty is to fight a dragon across yon field whilst ye maidens battle your own beasts. Luck, on the room, m'lady."

He chucked Lilly on her smiling chin. "Karita, my love, I'll be home to appreciate your labors with supper. We need to make wise choices, but I have the ultimate faith in you, my dear. I'll let you work your magic and create something amazing."

He doffed his ratty cap in another mock bow and ambled back into the store.

"Jerk." Kat said to his back, but he kept walking, pretending he hadn't heard.

He smiled to himself when he heard Lilly say, "Mom, that's not a nice word to call Dad. The teacher makes us take a time out if we say stuff like that."

He was out of earshot then, but he had to admit, he was digging this dad stuff. And the store had become so much more important than he'd expected. Honestly, he might not have bet against Kat when she mocked him for buying it, but now it felt...

right.

This was the glory he was looking for—a family, a place to call his own. Living in this town was never part of his plan, but he would compromise for the woman he loved.

Now he was coming into his own. People were accepting him. Saying hi on the street and asking his opinion about things. Jake didn't want to give a speech, but how much different could it be than jawing with the announcer in front of a Friday night crowd? He wasn't shy.

He had his own store where he made all the choices and investments. It would be his tail if he chose wrong. He didn't want Kat to know, but now he had all his money in it, and a sizable chunk of the tractors out back belonged to the bank. She'd doubtless think he was being a ridiculous dreamer.

Only thing was he'd asked Kat to help around the store, and she was bound to notice how heavily invested he was. He imagined her laughing at him for being so foolish. He'd have to keep her occupied and out of the books until he could prove he could make a profit.

Chapter 10

Lilly sat in silence on the way home, and Kat couldn't help but feel guilty for her behavior. It was hard to imagine her as a good mother when she couldn't even keep a civil tongue in her head. She was a jealous mother, that's what she was.

She glanced at Lilly, but the little girl stared out the window until they arrived at the ranch, then scrambled to start her chores.

Kat went to check with Eli about Potato Chip's condition and found the horse was comfortable, but now Milky Way was coming close to time to deliver her foal, so there was a new tension in the barn. Kat loved this part of her life, and Eli had more skill with the horses than the vet from the next town. She knew all would be well here.

"Don't worry, kid. She's a sturdy mare," Eli said. "She'll do fine."

Kat gazed around the barn, taking in the soft creaking of the wooden beams and the cozy warmth from the animals, remembering a zillion distinct memories that were created here.

"Eli, I just want to thank you for saving this for me..."

Kat tried not to tear up, mostly because Eli didn't cotton to bawling any more than Jake did. It just wasn't proper business to be spreading around emotional stuff, but she never followed their rules very well. "Do you think Jake and I have a chance to make this work?"

"You better, child. You got a lot of eggs in one basket now, so both you kids better act like ya'll done growed up. Lilly's counting on you, Kat. And so are they." He glanced at her belly. "I'm worried about you. I loved your mother something fierce. Despite her not being your blood kin, you're a lot like her. I just wish you weren't every bit as stubborn. It wasn't her best trait."

He smiled to lessen the insult, but Kat didn't need it. She knew Eli raised her to be independent. "I got all my hard-headedness from you. I know it sure as the sun will rise."

She looked out the loft window toward the chicken coop, wondering if Lilly had come back when she wasn't looking. She was supposed to be collecting eggs.

"Speaking of eggs in one basket, I'm going to check on Lilly. And Eli? Thanks again for looking out for me."

"What would I do with myself if I didn't have you to ride herd over? I'm fond of that young 'un, too. Guess you better get to tending her."

He made a shooing motion, and she chuckled, remembering when he would use that motion to send her to do her chores.

"All right. We're having a ham with mac and cheese for dinner. Come on up."

She enjoyed the content look on her grandpa's face. Kat wondered again how long until things went awry. She walked to the house to see if Lilly was already attempting to wash eggs, but there was no sign of her. She strolled down to the chicken house, but the girl wasn't there either.

With growing concern, she looked across the fields, then toward the riverbank. Panic set in. Just as she was about to alert Eli to help her look, she heard soft crying coming from the chicken house.

She opened the door and allowed her eyes to adjust to the dark, then she saw the compact figure huddled in the corner. Ignoring the fact it was the floor of a chicken coop, Kat sat next to Lilly, asking what was wrong.

"It's nothing." Lilly hiccupped over her tears but didn't lift her head from her knees.

Kat felt very guilty. "It's me, right? Because I yelled at Jake...

at your dad?"

"You don't really think of him as my dad. You don't even like him and you maybe won't even like me anymore soon. I've had lots of families that didn't want me anymore after they made their own babies. I'll have to go to a different home, and then... I don't want to leave."

The small girl wailed the last, then her body heaved with a wracking sob and Kat felt like she must have screwed up every parenting rule there could be. Why had she fooled herself into believing she could handle motherhood?

She gathered Lilly in her arms, letting her cry through the jag, then shifted her onto her lap so she could cry better. This was why she had fooled herself into believing it. Fake it 'til you make it. This girl needed her to try, and try she would. She would control her temper around Jake.

"Are you going to send me away?" Lilly asked. The small voice interrupted her thoughts, and she shuddered at the notion.

"Sweetie, I'm doing everything in my power to make sure you never have to leave. There are still some papers to be signed, but I love you as much as if I carried you in my belly. I didn't, and that makes what we have extra special. I carry you in my heart. We found each other because we needed each other. I've been foolish to be angry with your dad and I'll try to get it worked out, so you don't worry."

She smoothed dark hair and wiped red-rimmed eyes. "I've loved him a long time. I have a lot of love to give."

She nodded sagely. "That's what he said. You had enough love for the whole world. I just don't want it to end. I feel like, for the first time, life isn't so scary."

Digesting the statement, Kat hugged Lilly tight. "I hear ya, kiddo. Loud and clear." She stood, lifting Lilly to her feet. "So, what do you say we make Dad a special dessert, then we'll wait and let him help us make dinner?"

"Okay." Lilly squeezed her waist in a hug, then slipped her hand into Kat's.

The gesture was touching. Kat wanted her to have the advantages she had and have the mother she'd always wanted.

She was determined.

With a hesitant smile, Lilly asked, "So what kind of dessert will we make?"

The smile was reward enough, but that evening, things seemed to get better. Jake was distant with her, but he was great with Lilly and he seemed pleased they'd waited for him to start dinner.

Kat made a show of needing a big pot filled with water and placed on the stove. Lilly stood on a chair grating cheese while Kat melted butter in a skillet to sauté the ham Jake was slicing.

They worked together as a family. Though things seemed good, Kat was committing every moment to memory, just in case.

Eli came in and made a big deal of saying how he would set the table 'so they could get onto eating.' After supper, Lilly presented the strawberry shortcake she'd prepared mostly by herself and the guys claimed it to be the best they'd ever eaten. There was pride in Lilly's eyes and Kat hoped it would be the first of many chances to build her confidence.

Kat was content as she left Jake and Lilly to wash the dishes.

She stepped onto the back porch just in time to catch the last vestiges of light as the sun slipped over the hill. She had never been able to decide if she loved sunsets or sunrises more, but as often as possible, she tried to make time to watch them both to savor each day's random colors in her mind.

"Beautiful."

Jake's deep voice sent a tingle through her as he pushed open the screen door and stepped out, pulling the oak door shut behind him. She cleared her throat.

"I know. I still can't believe this whole ranch belongs to... us. When I was growing up, I always knew it would be mine someday but, standing here now..."

"Yeah. It's a great place, and it suits you, but I wasn't talking about the view of the ranch." He stepped over to the railing and stood close enough she could feel the warmth radiate from him. "You're prettier than sun up on a frosty morning. Whenever I doubt your awesomeness, I'm humbled by the person inside you, and I know I've never met a more beautiful woman."

"I don't know what to say... thank you. What are you talking about?"

Kat looked down at her worn boots and jeans, her worn flannel over a silly tee shirt that read in letters that were upside down, "If you can read this, flip me over and put me back on my horse." Nothing special. She possibly smelled like a chicken coop.

"She told you about the kids at school, huh?" Jake took off his ball cap, running his fingers through his hair as he glanced at her. "Lilly needed your help with that, so I'm glad you gals got things all figured."

"Hardly all figured out, but we talked through it. Thanks for picking her up today, looking out for her. All she talked about at dinner was driving that tractor." Kat moved fractionally closer to Jake, so she was touching him. He didn't step away.

"She's a natural, just like you. She's actually a lot like you, I noticed. Fate has a funny way of throwing the right folks together. Like us." Abruptly, he changed the subject. "I talked with Vivian and I think things are coming around, but I'm still worried about financing. I'm going to ask Lug..."

"That's not a good idea, Jake. I mean, how much funding are we talking? Fundraising I'm good at."

"I don't want you getting all worked up," Jake said. "Things are going to have to move quick-like now."

"I'm not made of porcelain," she said. "Seriously, if you don't stop telling me what I can't do, you're gonna see my sharp side."

"No way." He grinned at her, slinging his arm around her shoulder like when they were kids. "I could never get you riled."

He pulled back, robbing her of his warmth. "It's getting chilly. I'm going to watch TV with Lilly and Eli for a bit, then turn in. I have a big day tomorrow."

She watched him go, wishing he'd invited her. She heard laughter from the living room and realized the chilliness was more than in the air—it was also in her cold, lonely heart.

Things were going well for Jake. He left early that morning and she hadn't seen him, but he was slated to give a speech at six this evening. It was about ten 'til and the room was packed. Lana was next to her and had highlighted the bullet points of the speech she and Jake hammered out. It sounded simple enough.

"The best part was when I met with him, he'd already done most of the work," Lana whispered. "He asked my opinion on a few things, but he didn't beg me to do it for him like I expected. I told him it was free advice, just to mess with Viv. She was hoping to get some billable time out of him later. Something's different about him."

Lana hesitated, probing into Kat's soul with her bright green eyes. "Well, I guess you noticed since ya'll are finally shacking up again. Look, he's here." She nodded past the crowd at the door. "I wondered if he'd chicken out. Vivian has everyone in town here. Not an easy crowd for our own bad boy."

Kat was relieved as a murmur went through the crowd. When she saw him, she almost fell off her chair. Gone were his worn jeans, scuffed sneakers, and his infamous ragged ball cap. And his curls. He'd had his hair trimmed short in a sexy way she hadn't seen since high school. The man walking past her was... not Jake.

Well, so she thought until he doffed his old black Stetson at her and winked. Then she saw the crooked gleam in the back of his eyes that showed he was nervous. She recognized it as the same light that shone before he headed into an arena.

New jeans, a pressed shirt, a blazer... and his lucky boots. She thought they were gone forever. They disappeared from his hospital room when he had his accident and she thought he'd thrown them out.

He was wearing one of those crazy bolo ties his dad favored, and for the first time she could remember in forever, he was clean shaven. Somebody near the middle of the room let out a low wolf whistle.

Jake was handsome usually, but in a scruffy way, not this...

hunky way.

As Jake stood in front of the podium, he set his hat down in front of him on the papers he'd carried in. The rumbling around the room ceased in expectation. With a deep breath, her brave husband plunged in.

"Good evening, everyone. I'm excited to chat with y'all on this fine evening. I've only just come home to Riverbend Falls, but folks, I can tell you something. When I left this town a dozen years ago with the lovely Karita as my bride-to-be, I left behind something special. Now, I know there have been challenging times, and some folks moved off, but that special thing that was here when I left is still here. It's you."

He paused, looking around the room, making eye contact with several people. There was a light smattering of applause, but he held his hand up for quiet.

"As most of you know, I bought Hank's Hitchin' Post. Since then, I made a mistake. I suggested we should improve this town. Unfortunately, I said this to a particularly important woman, hence, here I am, tangled up in this mess."

His words were met with chuckles from the men and a variety of reactions from the women, including raised eyebrows and dissatisfied sniffs. With a look of disbelief, Lana shook her head at Kat.

"I did not write that," Lana whispered. "He's totally off track here. Vivian's gonna skin me."

"The key to making this town great again isn't to change anything, it's rediscovering our unique identity and embracing it fully. Our warm hospitality brings people back time and time again." Jake threw his arms out like he was running for president. "Let's do it like we used to, before Falls Mill opened."

His eyes landed on Lana, and Kat felt her body stiffen. Was he attacking what Lana was building? Garrett was on the other side of Lana, and Kat couldn't be sure, but he might have growled.

It had taken a lot of effort to get the town to support the idea of turning the historic Mill and campground into a resort. Their business would suffer if Jake moved sentiment the other way. Everyone loved Lana. What was Jake's angle?

"Here's the fundamental problem. We need to remind people we're here. The Harvest festival that used to draw folks in the fall is what we need."

"The Mill gets all the business. Folks have little reason to be in town except for floating and camping so far," someone called out. "Even that will dry up in the winter."

"Let's change that, make our street part of the experience people have when they come on vacation to Riverbend Falls. I propose a Harvest festival right here on Main Street. This year it will begin at my feed store. We'll work together, hopefully, with Falls Mill, and it will be publicity that will be good for all of us."

This time, it was clear who the dissenter was. Don Ragland, Park's dad, was a mean old cowboy, rumored to have been into cattle rustling in the early days. He had also competed against Lug Summers in the family rodeos back in the day, and the two men had a falling out.

He still bore animosity toward the Summers family.

"What do you think on this Main Street is going to draw folks in? Salt and sugar licks?" Don's nasty tone showed what he thought of the idea. "This is a ghost town."

Mrs. Goodwin stood up in the front and said, "Jake has the ghost in the barn. The allure of it has attracted curious visitors for years, and a Halloween festival featuring a ghost would be a hit." She sat down.

Renee stood up. "This has my support a hundred percent, and I hope other shop owners will contribute. I'll adorn my shop with festive decorations, and cute outfits for anyone shopping. And I'll be ready to pitch in wherever I'm needed. Someone needs to do something more than just talk in this town."

This time the applause was louder but still hesitant. Jake allowed a dramatic pause and Kat realized she was holding her breath, as anxious as the next guy to hear what he had to say.

"Also, the Summers Ranch will host a fundraising rodeo and the proceeds will go to cosmetic changes that have been brought to my attention, and if we raise a lot of money, which I know we can, folks, we'll buy kid's play equipment for the park."

He was killing it.

"Lug has agreed to announce the show and with his local reputation behind the mic and mine in the barrels, we should draw a fine crowd. I've also arranged for a few special friends to join us, and I suspect you'll know their names. Mrs. Bunsen, it should cover your awnings, and Sheriff Tate, your trash cans."

"That all sounds well and good, Jake, but most of us know what happened the last time ya'll hosted a rodeo." Don again. "We all got to watch your dad go nuts, yelling at you and your sister over the intercom. It wasn't a pretty sight. Who says your dad won't go berserk again? Even if he wasn't losing it, would he be sober enough to do the job?"

Oh crud. It would be downhill from here. Jake would fold. He wouldn't defend Lug on this. How had he thought he could do this without dragging his family through the muck?

"I say." The deep baritone was a mainstay in this town years ago, and everyone looked surprised to see Lug himself had slipped in the back door. If anyone had noticed before, it would have caused a stir.

"I say I won't screw it up because my son asked me to do this for him." He looked over at Don. "I hear ya. I know I've made a lot of mistakes over the years." He glanced at Tabby, but she was studiously avoiding looking at him. "We all have our crosses to bear."

He looked around, catching several of the older rancher's eyes. "I want to go ahead with this idea for two reasons. I want my boy to stay here and open Hanks because I, for one, don't enjoy driving to Crestview for feed."

Lug paused for dramatic effect, and Kat had to admit he certainly had everyone's attention.

"The second reasons obvious. The heart of this town was the hospitality of our business owners, the Mill which has recently been transformed, and our hometown rodeos. Let's bring back the rodeo and make the town's heart thump again."

The cheers were unanimous. The only people Kat could tell

in the room that weren't pleased were obvious.

Tabby wasn't having any. She excused herself and moved past Lug and out the door while everyone was erupting from their seats for the back-slapping.

Kat just sat there. Jake... back in the barrel.

"Quiet, folks. Just one more thing." Jake's commanding presence drew the room's attention, and the chatter died down. "What I meant by being louder was street festivals. Nature itself will bring people to see the fall colors, so let's plan to be waiting for them with an annual Harvest festival and see how it goes?"

"I'm in," Ralph hollered.

"Me too," Mrs. Bunsen cheered.

Jake's hand instinctively went to his head, and he appeared taken aback by the shortness of his hair. He picked up his hat and slipped it on. "For a start, as Riverbend Falls's newest business owner, I'll pledge to provide games and the hayrides on Halloween. Miz Harlow, if you provide some jams and jellies, I'll save booth space for it."

At her nod, he said, "Perhaps someone could organize one of those cakewalks?" His eyes went to where Tabby had sat, and Kat saw a brief flash of pain. Tabby would have managed all that for him, but Jake chose his father instead.

With Tabby, she was all in or all out.

"I'll help if you'll do a kissing booth!" Cynthia from the dress store called out.

Kat was so not fond of Cynthia, and that comment should have made her blood boil, but it barely penetrated.

"I don't know about that, folks. I'll leave that to a few party chairs that perhaps Vivian could appoint for us?" At her graceful nod, he said, "Then that's it, folks. From the Mill to Main Street, let the good times roll."

Kat just sat there as the meeting broke up.

Jake. Back in the barrel.

Chapter 11

Jake walked to where Kat sat a little while later. "That was great, huh? And I didn't even have to have help. Suddenly, I knew what to say."

Jake's smile was in place, but he doubted it reached his eyes. He was worried. He had read the signals. She was guarded.

"Can we back road home?" he asked. "Eli said he wouldn't mind to stay with Lilly if we took a little extra time getting back. I think we need to talk."

"I guess so," she said.

Despite her mechanical movements, she was still a breathtaking sight in her boots and jeans, and the thought of losing her made him feel sick.

Things took a turn for the worse when she laid eyes on his pickup parked out front after they stepped out the door. Her eyes bore into him with an accusatory glare.

"You didn't sell the truck? Did you lie? You've been planning to return to the circuit all along. How does this play? Jeering Jake back in the spotlight? Was that speech in there just fertilizer?"

He yearned to wrap his arms around her as her voice grew louder, imagining them sitting by the water's edge and opening up to each other.

"Kat, baby? Get in the truck, we'll talk, but not here in the street." The crowd had mostly dispersed, but a few curious individuals were moving closer to listen. "Paulo needed money, so I bought the truck back. For deliveries or driving you girls around... I'm not going to drive my family around on a motorcycle."

Kat hesitated. "Right, look. Sorry. That was just a lot to take in. It's cool." She shrugged and opened the passenger door, then slammed it shut without another word. Jake sighed deeply and walked around, climbing in to his old work truck.

She was undeniably his woman.

Jake was about to fire up the truck when the young woman Kat had seen at the Inn and Out knocked on Jake's window. When he saw who it was, he gave Kat a quick glance and got back out.

"Jake, honey, I thought that was you. We just got into town. I'm with Chuck, but he's already passed out in the motel room. What do you say you buy me a drink down at the river, for old times' sake? I was just going to figure out how to get there."

"Sam, ahhh, it's good to see you." Jake gave her a half hug, then leaned back against the truck. "I don't think so. I'm sure you can shake Chuck awake if you try."

She pouted, and it looked darling on her features. "Suit yourself, handsome." She glanced past Jake at Kat with a frown. "Hey, I remember you, don't I? You were the old lady who slipped past me and snaked him in Amarillo."

Jake groaned. "Don't be ridiculous, Sam. This is my wife, Kat."

The blond shook her head contemptuously. "Whatever. Your loss. It was good to see you, but I don't think we're sticking around. It's quiet. But who knows, I heard they had live music at this Falls resort place. If I don't see you around, feel free to look me up if you're out on the circuit. Good times."

She walked away, and Jake hopped in and had them headed in the other direction with a quickness. Kat breathed. Wow. Some nerve. Jake was there for her, but only just. Old lady?

Clearly, he had history with the hottie. Kat wondered how much history. Should she ask?

She was feeling hurt and didn't like it one bit. It was on her, though. He'd turned the babe down, but with hotties hunting him, how was he going to be content here? It wasn't his fault. He was just built for action.

Kat wanted to put her hands over her face and bawl. She'd tried to be generous, yet here she was jealous Jake was doing well. She didn't like him taking chances with his life, but when had he ever been any different?

How could she ask him to change the fabric of his life for her when he was trying so hard to do things she would approve of? How could she ask more of him than she was giving?

"Look, baby," Jake was staring straight ahead, but his tone was tender, "I'm not sure how to make things right between us, but I want to try. Why don't you start by telling me what's making those tears rain down your pretty cheeks?"

Kat choked back a sob, then took a deep breath. "Do you remember that day in the hospital when you said you were done with the rodeo? I believed you and I've always supported you, Jake—"

He harrumphed loudly enough that she paused.

"I have always tried to be supportive," she protested, "but I wanted you to be finished. Your dad's obsession with being the best drove your family apart, and I didn't want that for us. When I couldn't..."

She broke off. This hurt to say, and it would hurt to hear.

"Despite my deep longing for a family, the irresistible pull of the rodeo captured your heart. I'm afraid of what might happen if we don't work together to overcome our issues. I don't want to lose you. But I'm afraid."

He pulled the truck off the road onto the shoulder and scooped her into his arms while she cried. It had been so long since she tried to explain her feelings. She felt raw. How was it she could speak to any cause except her own fears and feelings?

"I'm afraid too. This life we created inside you... If it were to take you away from me and Lilly, we'd be lost without you. You're the peg we hang our hat on. I can't lose you. I need you, Kat."

Gentle lips kissed the top of her head, the side of her face, her lips. Tender. He was a balm for her soul. She would try harder to be honest—both with Jake and with herself.

Kat wasn't afraid of Jake being in the arena. She knew he was darn good at what he did—it was a fear of losing him to it. That fear had her backing away from her emotional investment in their marriage until she had hidden it from herself.

"I love you, Jake." She felt a rush of emotion as their lips met, and the rest of the world fell away.

He pulled back, brushing the hair away from her face. "Together, we can do anything. Speaking of, what do you say tonight we solve the problem of our separate bedrooms? I want you where I can touch you, hold you, feel the babies move. Let me lay by your side?"

She nodded her agreement, feeling a thread of genuine hope. Together, they could make it all work.

The next morning, Kat felt Jake slip out of bed and when she murmured sleepily, he leaned over, smoothing her hair, and dropped a kiss on her forehead.

"I have a surprise for Lilly today and I have to get it set up," he said. "I'll be back for breakfast."

He pulled his Levis over his boxers, slid his boots on, and was buttoning his shirt as he left. She let out a deep breath. The magic cocoon Jake created when he cradled her all night went with him, but she would remember the smurfy feeling all day.

She sat up, stretching her arms, and decided it was time to get up and going. Looking out the window, she saw the sky transforming from a deep blue to lavender, signaling the coming of the sun. The sound of the birds waking up drowned out any noise from outside, and she wondered what dragged Jake out of doors so early. She hopped up and dressed, seeking coffee.

The clattering of pots and pans filled the kitchen as she tinkered around, and an hour later, Lilly joined her. "Where's Dad? He said he had a surprise. Is it my own horse?"

Kat laughed. That had always been her own wish, and Eli had arranged for her to have several. Although she longed for a mother figure, she knew she was lucky to have Eli by her side. The idea hit her hard as she looked at Lilly, who was about to become a permanent part of her life.

Her world was full, and what she'd missed, maybe she didn't need.

"I'm not sure, sugar..."

Jake came in the back door, looking suspicious. "Is breakfast ready?"

Kat indicated the pancake platter on the table, and he grinned and pulled up a chair. "You are my kind of woman, Kat Summers." He gestured to the other chairs.

"If you ladies will help me demolish this stack, Lilly and I can get to the fun!"

So, this surprise didn't include her. Why would it? Being pregnant had turned her into a pariah. She felt the gentle swell of her stomach and decided it was worth it. She would just enjoy watching the two of them have fun with whatever Jake had cooked up.

"Let me set a few aside for Grandpa Eli, then you two devour away."

She nibbled at her own food as she listened to Lilly try to guess her surprise.

When Jake finished his plate, he told Lilly, "Go put on your oldest, junkiest clothes and shoes and hurry back."

The six-year-old bolted from the table and was back in a flash. She expected Lilly to wear the old worn-out shoes she'd been wearing to school, but instead she was wearing the new ones Kat had bought her. She noticed that Lilly, too, had a distaste for new clothes.

Like mother, like daughter.

Jake led his herd of curious females to the backyard, where hay bales were stacked strategically to create short walls. Kat looked at Jake, still confused until he brought out two air powered paintball guns.

She started shaking her head at the same time Lilly's eyes lit up. Leave it to Jake to do something foolish like this and make her be the bad guy for saying no way. Lilly would be a mess.

What if she got shot in the eye or something?

"You remembered," Lilly squealed. She looked up at Kat, her bright smile contagious. "The last place I lived there were two boys, and they had paintball wars all the time, but they wouldn't let me play. I've always wanted to try! I mean, how cool is this?"

Lilly ran out to inspect the hay bale course while Kat tried out her lecturing voice yet again.

"Jake..."

"I know what you're going to say." Jake reached back into the box behind him full of paintballs and pulled out a face mask that would cover Lilly's long hair and provide excellent protection for her eyes. "I want to give her this experience."

Kat relented. "Fine, you guys be careful. Do not shoot my freshly painted house or the barns or ya'll will spend the rest of your afternoon scrubbing it off."

She put her hand on her hip, giving him a solid stare, before calling out to Lilly, "Have fun, but be careful."

"Sure, Mom," Lilly said as she picked up a jar of paintballs. "Can I be green?"

Kat left them to their devices, realizing this was one game she would be glad to be left out of. She gathered laundry, tidied the dishes, and peeked out the back door at her nearly solidly spattered family. She would have to hose them off outside before she let them in.

The doorbell rang, and Kat started. Who would visit on a Saturday morning that would ring the doorbell? Most folks would walk around back and knock on the kitchen door. She dried her hands on a dishcloth and went to find out.

A very prim elderly woman stood there holding a clipboard when Kat opened the door.

"Karita Summers? My name is Madison Plum. We spoke on the phone last month. I'm here to check on Lilly's progress. May I come in?"

"Sure, please, Mrs. Plum," Kat said.

She had a terrible feeling about this. Lilly was a fluorescent rainbow and wearing the rattiest clothes she owned. How would this look like it was good for her welfare?

"Miss," the woman corrected.

She looked around the living room and nodded. Kat tried to see through her eyes. Outdated horse magazines overflowed from under the coffee table. There were cobwebs behind the TV.

She'd known the visit would be a surprise. She should have taken more pains...

"Mrs. Summers, I cannot help but notice it looks like you are with child. Do you feel that having a baby will impair your ability to treat young Miss Thompson as your own?"

"No!" Kat made herself not cover her stomach protectively in view of this dragon lady. "I already love Lilly as my own and she is fitting into this family perfectly."

"I see. That's good." She made some notations on her clipboard, and Kat wished she could see what she was writing. "Your husband... it doesn't say here what he does for a living."

Rodeo clown? Not exactly the type of job description that would get Jake extra brownie points. *Miss* Plum didn't look like she'd ever been near a horse, much less a rodeo.

Luckily, the hardware store was happening despite her earlier doubts. Jake was nearly ready to open. "He owns the local farm store, though we are still working toward the grand opening next weekend."

"So, he will be busy with a new career? Will you be putting in long hours at the store as well?"

Kat was feeling defensive. "I believe I'll be helping, yes, but Lilly will not suffer. She's like a fish in water at the store. She enjoys being there. However, I feel most of my time will be spent at the store while she's in school, so either Eli or myself will make sure she always has someone with her."

"Eli? Oh yes, the grandfather." She made notes on her clipboard and, as she kept scribbling, Kat leaned forward to see if she could make out the handwriting. Miss Plum met her eyes and lowered the clipboard. "Where is the child?"

"Uhm, playing out back with Jake." Oh dear.

"That would be the prospective Father?" She eyeballed the

clipboard and made a note. Kat hoped that was a good thing.

"Yes, well, Jake surprised Lilly with a paintball gun this morning so I have to warn you, both are quite... colorful."

"He bought a gun for a six-year-old?"

Disapproval showed clearly in her eyes. Kat felt the need to defend him, but wasn't sure what to say.

"A toy paintball gun, yes. And protective gear. Well, shall we go announce your arrival?"

Kat led the way through the house, and she could feel hawkish eyes evaluating everything they passed. She was glad she'd done the breakfast dishes.

In the backyard, a true battle was being waged. She almost hated to interrupt, knowing Jake's competitive streak would prompt him to ask Lilly for a rematch if they were interrupted. He hated a draw worse than he hated losing.

The visual onslaught clearly shocked Miss Plum. The two battle weary contestants looked surprised to see the elderly lady, but Jake appeared to realize what was happening.

"Ladies, anyone have a canvas? We are artists at work and we've lost our paper."

Lilly giggled, and Kat groaned. Jake always thought he was so funny, but Miss Plum did not look amused.

"I'm going to make some coffee for Miss Plum while you all wash up. I..."

"That won't be necessary, Mrs. Summers. I can tell you I'm an advocate of children playing out of doors, but I dislike the idea of children having access to dangerous toys."

Jake looked abashed, and Kat thought Lilly would cry.

"Please don't worry, Miss Plum," she said, "we took every precaution. We take gun safety seriously in this house. They're simply playing a game, surely you can see that. If you'd just..."

"I will, Mrs. Summers. I'll make a repeat visit before I offer my findings. It seems you all have quite a bit of cleaning up to do, so I'll be on my way out... for today."

She walked down the back steps and around the house. Kat looked after the woman with dismay.

She shouldn't have agreed to the paintball guns, but she had cut her own teeth on a twenty-two rifle when she was ten. Eli made sure she could shoot straight, clean her own gun, and that a dangerous snake wouldn't stand a chance. She kept that rifle in the stable for varmints.

If Miss Plum knew she believed in responsible gun training, would that disqualify her as a parent? Did she stand a chance now, anyway? Somehow, she doubted it. She didn't think the woman thought very much of their setup.

Just as she was about to chase after the woman and beg her to reconsider, Eli came around that corner of the house and got an eyeful of the two "artists."

He laughed so heartily Kat thought he would drop his walking stick. When he finally spoke, Kat wanted to hug him for bringing levity to the situation.

"So that's what had the old bird looking like she'd seen a bad horror movie." He slapped Kat's arm.

"Don't worry, I introduced myself as the responsible grandfather and tried to charm her a bit. I suspect she'll be okay. But you two... I don't know if ya'll will ever get clean. And by the by, don't you be putting those painted bales back in my barn, Jakob."

Eli hooted with laughter as he disappeared into the stable.

"I'm sorry, Mom," Lilly said, but Jake shushed her.

"Don't you be sorry, kiddo. We didn't do anything wrong. That old bird probably wouldn't know fun if it smacked her in the arm with a paintball."

Lilly smiled, but her shiny dark eyes were searching Kat's for reassurance.

"Enough of the old bird stuff, guys." Kat cleared her throat. "Well, unless you fancy a rematch, Lilly, I'd say you better finish your battle. Then you two get cleaned up and we'll see about lunch."

She left them to their game and went inside, sinking into a chair at the kitchen table with a glass of water, contemplating what to do next.

She refused to give up, and when she set her mind to save a cause, she rarely relented. Lilly meant so much more than a cause. Somehow, they'd figure out how to win over the unflappable Miss Plum, the old bird.

Chapter 12

As Halloween dawned, the sky burst into a colorful display of pinks and oranges. The sound of rushing water and chirping birds accompanied Kat as she decided on a walk down to the peaceful riverbank.

The scent of damp earth mixed with the refreshing smell of the nearby river, where the fall leaves danced over the water in the morning sunlight. It was beyond breathtaking.

As she breathed in the brisk air, she felt the excitement that seemed to have captured the entire town. In just a few hours, she'd join Lilly and Jake in character and off they'd go to Jake's Hitchin' Post for the start of the festivities. She liked that he'd changed the name of the store when the rest stayed mostly the same. It made it more real to her.

She could almost hear the local bands playing festive music and the chatter of the crowd as she imagined the Halloween celebration on Main Street. Jake had been working around the clock to be ready to open for business today and, as much as possible, everything was in place.

Lilly was the most excited of all. She had chosen her own costume, and tried on the cowgirl gear three times this week, "just to make sure it was functional," Lilly had said.

At only six years old, she carried herself as if the weight of the world was on her small shoulders, and Kat could sense her self-consciousness. But she was clearly having fun.

Jake and Lilly teamed up to decorate the store, assuring Kat that everything was going smoothly. They worked together well, a father and daughter duo.

They'd transformed the barn into a spooky wonderland, with pumpkin bowling, pumpkin painting, and other Halloween-themed games dreamed up by the two, and even though they'd let her see it, they'd wanted it to be a surprise, so had left her out of the planning. According to Lilly, surprising Kat would be better than having a party.

As the wind picked up, Kat shivered and pulled her jacket tighter around her, feeling the chill of the morning air off the water. But the thought of their adoption failing sent a different kind of shiver down her spine.

She'd listened in on Jake and Lilly's conversation about the new babies last night, and heard the fear in Lilly's voice, despite Kat's attempts to reassure the girl.

Kat's eyes brimmed with tears. Then and now. What Jake said was exactly what Lilly needed to hear. While their communication was honest, Kat couldn't shake the feeling that she was being left out of their growing bond. Her heart ached with the weight of her loneliness.

Determined to shake off any petty feelings plaguing her, she walked for a while and caught sight of the wild stallion across the river. The sight of his glossy coat and muscular build brought a smile to her face. Though he was young, he ruled his herd with an iron hoof. After the ice storm, she'd noticed a shift in the herd's pecking order, with him moving up.

She felt the anticipation build as she watched the stallion cautiously approach the water. He leaned his long neck in and took a drink, watching her. Then, with a frisky toss of his head, he galloped back towards the rest of the herd, kicking up a cloud of dust behind him.

Forgetting her sadness, she sat down, resting her back against a large rock. She laid her hand across her stomach, feeling oddly content as she watched the antics of some of the younger horses. She had done this. Not her alone, of course. It had taken a coalition, but these horses were free and safe because she helped them. She was good at helping people or animals that couldn't help themselves.

Maybe that was why she had so much trouble with Jake over the years. He was so strong and smart, so capable. She loved being with him, but somehow, she felt less. She picked a blade of fescue from beside her.

It wasn't Jake that made her feel this way—it was her.

He believed she was intelligent and competent, and she knew it. He told her so, and sometimes she listened. Her self-criticism was at its harshest when she was angry, though, so that made it her problem to solve.

How to let it go? It felt ugly to be jealous. According to Jake, it wasn't a good fit for her. She'd tried to hide it, but he knew her better than she knew herself sometimes.

As the size of their family increased, she pondered whether Lilly felt the same way? She had said she was afraid the babies would make her unwanted.

Some kid put that notion in her head, and Jake had casually mentioned it when they were alone. Jake had become Lilly's confidant, maybe because he never judged her. It was heartwarming to see how naturally Jake had taken to being a dad. She had to believe the three of them could do this.

Kat had started too many fights to count because he couldn't see beyond his own ideas and refused to discuss starting a family. She could see he'd been right at that stage in their life, if she admitted it to herself. Meeting Lilly was a turning point for Kat. The hodgepodge group she was attached to finally formed a family. She certainly wasn't jealous of Lilly.

Grateful was more like it.

Getting pregnant was a mistake, one she wouldn't take back for the world, but if something bad happened and she was... endangered again, Jake would never forgive her, and she doubted Lilly would either.

So, she'd have to be ridiculously careful. She was determined to stay with them. She'd made promises.

All the reasons it wouldn't work in her mind crumbled if she allowed herself to believe. They were already a family, and she knew that nothing worth having would come easy.

Watching until the horses drifted away, she stood up thoughtfully, her butt numb, and took a deep breath of the river fresh air. The time had come for her to go join her family.

There was to be a lot of action that day, and with a lighter heart, Kat climbed the hill to the house, eager for the festivities to begin.

A little while later, she slipped into her slinky costume, careful to not mess up the whiskers she'd painted on her cheeks. She pinned the tail on the back, slid the headband with cat ears over her dark hair, and looked in the mirror. Kat opted for simple flats rather than the boots that would have catapulted her from cute cat to Catwoman, but it was okay. She was a mom now.

The smiling reflection looking back at her was nice. The pregnancy had put a shine on her complexion. If someone could bottle that and market it, they would make a fortune.

She picked up her old Polaroid camera from the dresser that spawned her love of photography as a girl, thoughtful. She used to always have a camera. That might be something she needed to bring back.

She gave a last swish of her tail in the mirror and went to see if everyone else was ready. Jake was.

Man, she married a real hottie. Breathe. Yum!

He wore a long black cape with a red lining draped over his lean shoulders and a light powder dusted his skin, making him seem translucent. He made fangs sexy.

Lilly clomped down the stairs at the same time Eli came in the back. Eli's cowboy costume wasn't much of a stretch. If he hadn't secured the toy guns to his hips instead of his real varmint holster, Kat wouldn't have known him from a regular workday.

Lilly was hilarious. Gone was her carefully chosen western shirt and boots, and in place was the crude costume of a rodeo clown. Mismatched socks, the infamous painted sneakers she wouldn't give up after the paintball war, hankies hanging everywhere. Her face was painted white with a big red smile.

She even had a rubber nose, and if she wasn't mistaken, it was Jake's lucky nose.

"You changed your costume?" Kat loved it, but Lilly had been proud of her other one.

"Yep." She spun around. "Isn't this great? You know, I watched a rodeo yesterday with Dad on TV and he told me the clown has one of the hardest jobs there. Grandpa had plenty of these hankies, so I made a new costume. Isn't this cool?" Her eyes were waiting for approval, and Kat had no trouble giving it to her.

"You look purrrfect darling! Well, are we ready to stir up some mischief in the heart of Riverbend Falls, my motley crew?"

With smiles and cheers, they set off, Jake driving Kat and Lilly in his truck, and Eli the authentic cowboy mounted his horse, and he and his dog followed at their own pace.

The town was full-blown fun. There were booths set up around selling cider and candied apples. There were children in costumes streaming around with balloons and cotton candy, bags of candy and loot being hauled around by their parents. Not too many adults had dressed in costume, but overall, it looked like a great turnout.

They parked at the Hitchin' Post and Lilly was giggling in the back seat. Jake turned around to look at her after he took in the large hand painted Grand Opening sign that hung across the business front. "Did you have something to do with this?"

"Mom helped me, but we thought if you had a big sign, everyone would come." She fixed him with a serious gaze. "If you make a lot of money, maybe you can afford all of us."

He burst out laughing and unhooked his seat belt. "Kiddo, I wouldn't give you up for love or money. Stop worrying your head about that nonsense. You're a Summers now, kid."

Kat watched the scene and wondered how he was so easy with Lilly. He always said the right thing, well, unless he was talking at her. Then somehow things tended to get out of hand.

There would be none of that today. It was a day of celebration. After getting out of the car, Kat hugged Lilly tight, savoring the warmth of the girl's embrace before she vanished into the store with Jake.

Her family. Looking around at all they'd accomplished in town filled her with intense pride. Mrs. Bunsen's new awnings were navy and teal, and the old gal was wearing a costume resembling a queen sitting on a stool, set up with some of her jewelry in a booth beside her for sale.

Looked like a young couple were browsing the rings.

Kat followed Jake and Lilly inside, where Jake had everything organized and well stocked, everything from nuts and bolts to grain bins and seed bins to his new western wear section.

He'd added a big freezer in the back, with plans to buy and sell beef, and he'd bought into a company that sold greenhouses. There was a new show model erected out back by the barn that he'd purchased to start and sell plants next year.

He'd branched out to fill the need. Impeccable strategy. It would help Falls Mill, and it would make caring for her horses much easier.

Jake clapped his hands together. "Well, gang, is everyone ready?"

A chorus of yeses answered, and it was time to man their stations. All stores would be open for business from 12 to 4, then they would close and take part in the costume contest and chili cook off Falls Mill was presenting.

Jake and Tabby would man the store, and Lilly would help the volunteers in the "haunted" barn with the games. Kat was going to play photographer at the "photo with a ghost" backdrop until the stores closed.

Jaime's husband, Tad, offered to drive the large tractor and trailer retrofitted with hay bale seats for twenty. Anyone could ride, whether you were staying at Falls Mill or just floated down the river and wondered what all the signs were about. They already had three full trailer rides booked prior to the event, so Lug offered to help him out.

Garrett was at the park with Lana hosting the cook off, and Jaime had stayed behind at the Mill to make sure everything went smoothly there. The gang was all here, but not quite back together.

Kat looked at her camera, thinking of how many hundreds of pictures she took of the four of them, Jake and Jaime and her and Lana. Times were good.

She'd gone digital long ago, but she loved her old Polaroid for a quick hard copy. Her photoshoot was a clever use of the paint spattered hay bales as a backdrop, and she had a feeling that the "ghost" would catch the attention of some curious individuals.

The photos would cost a dollar to cover film costs, but she planned to donate the money to the restoration fund Jake started at the bank. Everyone was talking about the ghost and there was already a line at her station.

A very live looking dummy was their ghost, slightly hidden by a gauzy sheet. A small fan blew the sheet gently, and it gave the dummy a sense of shadowy movement. Suspended above the ground, he was wearing the flannel shirt and bib overalls that he allegedly wore in past sightings. It made a pretty dramatic backdrop, and she stayed busy for a while. Thankfully, she'd brought extra film.

When her lines finally dwindled, she took a deep breath. She leaned against the rickety old building for a moment as a little dizzy spell visited. Doubtless, just too much excitement. She reminded herself she was being sensible and decided to just sit for a while.

Hayrides had been bringing people up from the river to the festivities all day, and Falls Mill's booth over at the park had the air already smelling so good. She knew the chili cook off was bound to be a raising a decent little chunk of donations.

Lilly came back and said she didn't want to play any games. By the time she'd hung out for an hour, several kids had asked her to play. Kat urged Lilly to go, cautioning her to stay within eyesight of the barn, where several of the older gals were running the games, and to check in with her every thirty minutes.

After Lilly left, Sheriff Tate came by and gave Kat grief about allowing Lilly to ride in the back of the truck last week. Apparently, he'd seen them from the river where he was fishing, so he thought he'd use this opportunity to remind her of the rules of the road. The man was a pain.

"Thank you for pointing that out, Sheriff, but I know full well you haul things more illegal than kids in the back of your truck. Eli said you offered him fresh deer meat just the other day. Bow season's not for what, another month or so?"

He was a well-known hunter, and despite being a lawman, she knew he might get a deer out of season for the meat. He seemed sorry for the harassment, but he wasn't finished.

"So, I saw Jake in the hardware store. A dozen years ago, he practically kidnapped you, and we haven't seen him since. Do you think we'll forget about that?"

"It's called eloping, Sheriff. It's what happens when two people love each other and don't want to deal with the sometimes unkind opinions of others about the person they love. You might try falling in love. You could discover there's a reason not to be grumpy all the time."

"Hmph." He patted his considerable girth. "Your grandfather wasn't happy—so whatever ya want to call it. I don't know what I'm worried about. I'm betting that boy won't make it two months." He tipped his Stetson at her. "Kat, look out for yerself. I heard... well. Just remember, a polecat doesn't change his stripes."

Kat rolled her eyes as he walked away. Luckily Sheriff Tate was too lazy to ranch so he wouldn't hurt Jake's business, long as he kept his mouth shut. Fat chance of that.

He actually might be laying odds on a bet, another one of his questionable habits. Most of the old men got into those private bets, and it wasn't illegal, but the man was an officer of the law.

When he'd arrested them that New Year's Eve, the entire course of her life changed. Yep, she'd remember, a skunk stinks even if he doesn't have a white stripe.

Despite the crimp in her mood, she put on a smile and got to work with several large family groups who wanted individual photos. Not in the booth—with the feed store. Oh well, a buck was a buck.

By the time she got another break, Lilly had checked in twice and now she was staring at Cynthia, her least favorite person in town.

"I don't mean to tell you your business," she said, "but I would think until you actually got that child adopted, you'd keep a closer eye on her."

Cynthia ran a dress shop down the stretch from the Hitchin' Post that no one could really afford to shop at. She was always sticking her nose in everyone's business and acting all high and mighty about it.

Kat glanced around the parking lot full of people. "Lilly is supposed to be playing games in the barn."

"She's on the bench out in front of the store. Lilly looks likely to follow the same path you've taken." Cynthia sighed and shook her head. "It's a shame how often young love ends in tragedy, though."

Kat put up her closed sign and picked up her camera. Lilly was late checking in, but it wasn't likely she was causing trouble out in front of the store. But she didn't check in, so Kat was a little concerned.

It was after 3:30 and the square likely had twice as many people as an hour ago. Many from neighboring towns, some she recognized, some not.

"Thanks for your concern, hon. As far as love goes, I'd think you'd have to know before you could judge." Well, that came out mean.

The classy clothes Cynthia wore couldn't soften the ugliness of her sneer. "Whatever."

"Enjoy the rest of your day, then." Maybe Kat could brush her off more nicely. "The thought of the warm, savory chili is making my mouth water. The buzz is that Ed Rosati and Doc Robbins will face off against each other. That should be a tough competition. You should head on over so you get a bowl."

"Do you know who else is in the contest, a late entry? Lug Summers. This guy can't even pump gas without being drunk, but suddenly he thinks he can have rodeos again and speak at the council because of Jake's new found fame? That's just nuts."

She looked like she was gonna faint from the scandal and started patting her chest.

Can't possibly get that lucky.

She seemed to have no idea she was talking about Kat's family, but of course she did. That was the thing with small town life, love it or hate it. Everyone knew everything and would give you their opinion if you'd hold still long enough.

She wasn't going to hold still any longer.

"Good day, Cynthia."

She strode off, cutting through the crowd toward the front of the store. There was a small worry niggling at her. Lilly was late to check in and what if... she was just six. How did she lose track of her daughter with all these extra folks in town? Seemed highly irresponsible.

Luckily, Lilly was just sitting on the old timers bench in front of the store with a boy about her age, watching everyone walk by. Relief flooded Kat. Geez, this parenting required her to use hindsight for foresight. She'd have to stay in front of the curve.

As the little boy took Lilly's hand, she felt a sense of impending doom. For heaven's sake—six—way too young to be thinking about boys!

"Lilly, you're late checking in."

The fact both kids jumped a mile high meant Kat wasn't overreacting. Whoa. Okay, getting a grip on it.

"You can invite your friend to sit with us at the cook off, but it's past time for you to have checked in. You were supposed to stay by the barn." There were chaperones there.

Dang, she didn't notice that Jake was hot until she was fifteen.

"Sorry, Mom. This is Kevin. He's new in my class."

Lilly jumped up and pulled Kevin up beside her, and gave him a hug, her red nose falling to the ground. He leaned down and picked it up, and Kat saw tears in his eyes.

"Kevin, it's a pleasure to meet you," she said with a soft smile. "Are you here with your parents?"

"No, ma'am. My Grandma Goodwin. My parents... well,

they don't get along anymore, so I'm going to live with Grandma until my Mom comes for me." He swiped his nose with a sweater that was unraveling.

Oh. Esther Goodwin was a wonderful lady with cats, but she hadn't realized the woman had children, let alone a grandchild. It wasn't likely she had a lot of experience with kids. "Are you having a good time today, Kevin?"

He shook his head. "I was glad to see Lilly since she's nice to me at school, but we were just talking about what a bummer it is that I can't be in the costume parade with her."

Hmm. "Well, if you think your Grandma would be okay with it, you could spend the afternoon with us. Perhaps we could find something at the store to make into a costume."

"Yeah. I need a cowboy to save," Lilly said. "My Dad has everything in the store and he knows all about cowboys. He can tell you what to do."

The young man's eyes lit up. "Really? My Grandma won't mind but I'll ask. She's over there talking to Lilly's grandpa."

He ran over while the two girls waited. Esther waved her cane and Eli his staff as Kat herded the two children up the steps to the feed store.

When Lilly reached out and took Kevin's hand to hurry him along, Kat breathed a sigh of relief. Perfectly normal childlike behavior, not the budding romance that makes parents crazy.

Chapter 13

The morning's carefully placed displays and decorations were now a jumbled mess. Wondering if an angry mob vandalized the store, Kat hurried to find Jake working a line at the register, side by side with Sam, the buckle bunny from the other night.

"Bless the light, you're here." Jake reached for the ball cap that wasn't on his head because he was wearing a cape instead. His make-up was streaked, and he looked stressed. He came around the counter, giving her his full attention, while Sam chatted with the guy buying a shovel.

Kat pondered the shovel, wondering if she needed it to hit Jake with. Why was this gorgeous blond standing at his hip? Why hadn't he called her? She tried not to let it hurt.

"I haven't had a single second, and Mom got wind of something at the park earlier, had her flying out of here." Jake's desperate blue eyes locked onto hers as he shook his head.

"I need to go find out what's going on, and I also need to hook up an extra trailer for the hayrides back to the Mill because we have a lot of bodies, and they are all gonna want to leave at once. I'm slammed and I'm running behind."

Kat looked at the line. Men holding hammers, machinery belts, ax handles. They were looking at Jake like he was a choice steak and she had a feeling curiosity fueled the onslaught more than a desperate need for new hammers.

"Better yet, the kids and I will hook up the tractor and you and your bunny finish up here, then we'll just head to the park together." She looked around.

Despite her green-eyed monster, she could see the empty shelves proving amazing first day sales. She had been worried, knowing he must have sunk most of his money into this. He hadn't asked her for a dime. She felt a swell of pride for her man. She glanced at the pretty blond watching them along with a half dozen old timers.

"Kids?"

"I'll explain in a few minutes. It's almost four, darling." He shifted his attention back to his customers, who were perhaps hoping for a show. She stroked his arm. "Almost there."

"Okay, but be careful with the tractor. Don't strain on the hitch."

He moved back behind the counter and missed the dramatic roll of her eyes. As if she needed advice about hooking up a tractor.

She looked around for the kids and followed the sound of giggling to the area of western wear Jake had asked her to stock. They were sitting on the floor with an odd assortment of garments. Kevin was holding suspenders.

"Mom, can I do chores to buy these things? Kevin is going to be a clown like me. We worked out some jokes."

"Yeah, Mrs. Summers. Lilly's funny."

Kat loved her daughter just a little more, proud she had a kind heart. She wondered what kind of jokes six-year-old clowns would tell, but hesitated to ask.

"We'll work something out, sweetie. I'm sure your dad will let you do some extra chores around here."

Lilly gathered the things and stood, Kevin in her shadow. She shoved the things in his arms and pointed toward the bathroom. "Change in there, then my dad can help you with pointers, like he did me."

Kat adjusted her ears, then kissed Lilly on the top of the head.

"I'm going out back to set up the tractor for the hayride. You guys wait right here. I'll be back in five."

She noticed the line dwindling when she hurried out the back door and was pleased to see Sam apparently waving goodbye as she headed out the front.

Kat hopped on the tractor Lilly had driven last week and backed it up to a secondary trailer where they'd thrown the extra bales of hay after designing the seats. It wouldn't be pretty, but they were seats. Climbing down, she quickly attached the hitch and then pulled the tractor alongside the store.

Hopping off, she had to steady herself as the feeling of lightheadedness washed over her. She leaned against the large tire for support, praying Jake wouldn't come looking for her. She would tell him tomorrow, today was his big day.

Kat realized the dizzy spells were coming more often, and the notion made fear claw at her belly. She had a long way to go in this pregnancy and hoped this wouldn't be one of the wicked side effects.

Jake was going with her to her checkup on Monday. Things were changing. She would take it easy and let the pampering grow on her.

Kat crossed the back lot to the store, and she felt fine by the time she got to the door. She was undoubtedly just being silly, but she'd feel better after she shared with Jake.

For now, they had an hour of hay rides and bobbing for apples at the park before the costume parade and the cook-off finale. So, Lug had entered... she wondered if Jake knew yet.

Jake was dead tired. The day was a blur of activity and craziness. It was spot-on for Halloween. He figured the gates of the underworld would likely open and pull him in.

His mom had ditched him early on, and every farmer and rancher for twenty miles came in to grill him. Luckily, mostly everyone bought something, but it had taken several weeks to stock and he wasn't ready for another onslaught on Monday.

Hopefully, every day wasn't like today.

If only he had his hat. The costume had been a rotten idea.

He'd been roasting like a hog at spit. Being dressed as a bloodsucker had warranted several remarks about him and Kat and he'd had to bite his tongue to keep from lashing out at the lackwits, but he'd been too busy to snipe.

Then Sam had come in and slipped right in next to him, chatting with the customers and letting him ring stuff up without talking. He'd been gonna text Kat, but he just never could get to his phone. It was innocent on his part.

Sam mentioned that she and Chuck had argued again and were leaving. She wanted to say goodbye and had a few minutes to help. He was onto her scheme. The absence of his wife was only a bait to Sam, but it didn't matter. She meant nothing.

Sheriff Tate was the worst with his bias, but he didn't matter in the scheme of things, either. Kat knew he'd done this with his own money and reputation. He wasn't a drifter... anymore. Jake was a family man now. He'd earned his way and had a way to provide for his family.

Jake had become fixated on the cost of raising two babies at once, so a good opening day was a boon, but he still hoped most days wouldn't be like this one. He locked the front door and heard Lilly's laughter in the back.

Time to find out what was going on with her and the scamp who'd been holding her hand. Wasn't she too young to hold a boy's hand?

The scene around the corner was unbelievable—two rodeo clowns and a feisty cat.

He chuckled. "Kat, honey, do you realize you're a cat?"

"Of course I'm a cat, I..." The irony hit her at the same time it did the kids, and they collapsed in a heap of giggles.

"Kat's a cat, Kat's a cat," Jake teased.

She smirked. "Says the man who dressed as a bloodsucker for his grand opening."

That was a little too close to what the sheriff said and he started to bristle. Kat shook her tail at him and the pleasant view changed his mind. They needed to get a move on.

"Let's go have our own personal hayride to the park, guys," said Kat. "Dracula, you'll be the purrrfect driver."

She led the way with a feisty shake of her tail.

"Lilly, have you ever bobbed for apples?" Kevin asked. "I can show you how." He threw his arm around her shoulder and they followed Kat out the back door.

Jake followed, determined to keep an eye on the young man putting the moves on his daughter. He fired up the tractor hauling his family, then drove down Main Street, stopping to pick up folks on the way to the park at the other end of the street, just for the novelty.

He knew the upcoming family drama would be worse than a nightmare about the gates of Hades, but he was out of people to offer rides to.

Lug had entered the chili cook-off, and so had Tabby. He had no idea why his parents were making fools of themselves. They were putting on a show, and it was obvious they were getting out of hand.

Tabby was alternating sniping at and ignoring Lug, whose table was next to hers. If one of their recipes beat the other, Jake was worried about open war.

Too bad Jaime was at the Mill. He wondered if she'd had the good sense to offer to stay there because she knew what their folks were up to. He needed her. She could wrap their father around her finger—if she wanted to.

No, Jaime wasn't here, and he wished he wasn't either. Despite the cheerful noises his crew was making over their chili samplers, watching his parents made him remember why he avoided this town.

He wished they would act with more dignity. Sometimes he was sorry for them because he knew they still loved each other. Just no way one would let the other prevail.

Jake hoped Doc Robbins won the cook-off, but as he tasted the soupy texture, he knew either of his parent's subtly different recipes would be better. Ed Rosati was an excellent cook, and his Italian was legendary, but it was tough to judge it better than either of his folk's recipes. Maybe fate would be kind and there would be a tie.

"All right everyone. The judges have made their decision."

Vivian waved from the grandstand where the four tasting stations were. "First, let's do the costume walk. Everyone in costume, please line up, then we'll parade across the stage."

She paused while princesses and monsters hurried to the line, and Kat was pleased to see a few other spirited adults in costume. Lilly and Kevin had their heads together, whispering their jokes.

"Okay everyone," Vivian called out, "let's have applause for these clever costumes."

Light applause filled the park then turned into hoots of laughter when Lilly stopped center stage and called out to Kevin, "Hey, did you know you can pick your friends and you can pick your nose, but you can't pick your friend's nose?"

"Well, did you know you can tune a piano, but you can't tuna fish?" Kevin called back. He made an attempt at a cartwheel and Lilly managed a slightly better one. Then the two somersaulted to the other side of the stage. The applause was deafening.

"Did you have anything to do with those jokes?" Jake asked. She shook her head. "You?"

"Nope, so that was all them. That's our girl up there."

Jake found himself grateful for the life Kat had sprung on him. If Lilly was not the product of Jake and Kat's own genes, she certainly was doing a good job of seeming like it.

A regular daddy's girl.

"What do you think will happen if Vivian announces Tabby or Lug the winner?" Kat whispered.

"World War Three," Jake answered dryly.

When Ed Rosati was announced the cook-off winner, Jake breathed a relieved sigh. The prize was a weekend in a cabin at Falls Mill, and Ed Rosati was looking slyly at his wife Kendra as he waved his prize envelope. His parents were glaring at each other, but they were shaking hands and nobody's head got stuck in a pot of chili...

Hours later, Lilly was asleep between them and they were almost home. Kat had removed her ears and loosened her hair. Jake's face paint was itching, and he was dying to get out of his costume, but he couldn't help thinking how much he'd rather take Kat out of hers.

He reached across the back of the seat and squeezed her shoulder. "That was beyond my wildest dream, Kat. I couldn't have done it without you girls."

"I didn't help much. It seemed like you managed everything. You're amazing." Kat thought hard. "And I'm not mad that you had a friend step in and help. It's cool. I'm going to trust you."

Her sweet voice was as delicious as her words. How rare for her to be proud of him.

"I want to make you proud of me for the rest of our lives, babe. I can do this."

"When I saw your parents up there..." Kat paused.

"It's okay. I know how they are. I just wish they'd just get along and I hate talking about it. How can it help? You can just watch them and know it's hopeless."

She squeezed his hand. "Don't say that. I would have said a month ago there was no hope for us and look at us now. A family on the way home from the successful husband's grand opening. I couldn't be happier, darlin.' I know we can win over Miss Plum and this family will be strong."

She released his hand and rested it on the slowly growing curve of her belly. "We can do this," she whispered desperately.

It was total crap. He felt a knot in his stomach as he thought about what could happen to her. This was sketchy, and he was just fooling himself.

He felt like a terrible husband for doubting her body's ability to carry the kids. He wanted to be wrong. They pulled into the driveway and he uttered up a silent prayer to watch over his family.

He lifted Lilly out of the center of the truck to carry her in. She snuggled into him. "I love you, Daddy." He'd never heard words so precious.

"I love you, too, kiddo," he admitted. Kat looked into his eyes, her own shining with tears, and he felt like the luckiest man on earth.

"Well, let's get inside," Kat said. She gestured to the light in the stable loft. "Looks like Eli and his horse made it home safe."

Jake chuckled, trying not to disturb Lilly as he carried her inside. "I'd hate to be the fool that crossed that tough old crow."

Kat watched as Jake set Lilly on her bed and roused her. "Time to jammy up and jelly tight, kiddo. Don't forget to brush your teeth." He stood and ruffled her hair.

"I'll be down after I get a quick shower if ya want to visit over a bowl of ice cream," Kat said. "Feel up to it?"

"I couldn't eat another bite," Jake said, "but I'd love to watch you eat it. See ya soon."

Kat moved to help Lilly with her pajamas and Jake closed the door behind the two most important gals in his life.

He intercepted Kat outside her bedroom door.

"Babe?" His voice was deep and trembling with an emotion he tried to conceal, but he feared she'd see the longing in his eyes. "Mind if I join you in the shower? I haven't washed your hair in so long and..."

"I can't refuse such a charming offer," she murmured, her eyes sparkling with excitement as she pushed the door open and closed it behind him.

She undressed, the slinky black pantsuit pooling at her nearly naked feet. The only thing she was wearing were the two little scraps of Halloween colored silk she'd bought a few weeks ago. He'd doubted he would ever see her wrapped in them and—whoa. Jake couldn't help but feel a rush of desire as she led the way to the shower.

"Good heavens." With a sigh of relief, Jake shed his costume. He followed, determined to tend her. His wife was a dream.

Sex is completely off the table, dude. Bummer.

Chapter 14

Kat woke from a terrible dream as cramps wracked her body. Quietly, not wanting to disturb Jake asleep beside her, she curled into herself and tried not to cry out.

Another pain, a horrible spasm that left her reeling, then it was gone. She waited, praying the pain was over, and it was.

She sat up, thinking to splash her face when she felt it. Blood. She knew the sticky feeling immediately and a hoarse cry pried itself from her lungs. Her simple nightgown was soaked in blood.

Jake turned on the bedside lamp. "What is it, babe? Are you okay?"

She was sitting with her back to him when she heard his sharp gasp. He'd seen the blood. "I can feel it, Jake. I lost them." Tears were streaming down her face.

"Oh no, Kat. No."

She felt his hot tears mingling with her own as he pulled her to him, cradling her. Kat wished he wouldn't touch her. She felt tainted, incapable... she should have confessed about the lightheaded episodes she'd been having. This was all her fault.

Not Jake's. He'd practically immobilized her, not allowing her to do anything that amounted to anything. Jake hadn't even wanted to have sex last night, though she'd told him Doc

Robbins said it was okay if they were careful. He just held her and her heart was so full. Now empty.

"Let's get you to the hospital." He picked up her cell and speed dialed Doc Robbins, letting him know what happened. Doc was going to meet them at the hospital in Crestview. Jake cleaned her up and bundled her into the car, calling Eli to come and stay with Lilly.

Kat was silent. What was there to say? She felt worthless, but at least she didn't die. Just her babies. The tears wouldn't stop.

"Please stop crying. It could be something else. You don't know for sure you miscarried. What if..." He fell silent and Kat didn't reassure him. She knew. There was nothing that could be done. Her heart sank as she saw the crimson stains on the sheets, knowing that it was all that was left of their unborn children.

"I'm sorry," Kat sobbed. She clutched at her waist, wishing something could have been different. What was wrong with her? "This is my fault. After last time..."

Jake's voice was tortured. "Please don't do this to yourself, Kat. It wasn't your fault—either time. Sometimes things just don't work the way we want them to."

"I knew I hadn't been taking my birth control religiously when I came to see you. I didn't get pregnant on purpose, but some part of me wanted it so bad, and I was so sure I wouldn't fail again." An empty sensation crept over Kat, leaving her feeling numb.

"You didn't fail, love. You're here." Jake reached over and squeezed her hand. "Let's wait until we see the doc, okay?"

"It won't matter. I lost Melody, and now I've lost the twins. We were going to be a family, Jake." Kat's voice was shrill, and she wondered if she was hysterical.

His hard voice grounded her a bit. "We are a family, Kat. You, me, Lilly, and Eli. We need you in that family. If the babies weren't strong enough to make it into this world, I'm sorry, honey. It's painful to think about the life we couldn't give them, but I'm thankful that you weren't taken from us as well."

He put his hand on her arm, glancing away from the road

briefly. "I need you, babe. Your family needs you. If it wasn't meant to be, please accept it—and let it go."

"My heart feels like it's torn into a million pieces," she cried.

"What you did to me when we... lost Melody, that's what it feels like to have your heart torn into a million pieces. You shut me out, left me all alone with my grief. You say I'm too daring on the circuit, but you know what it feels like to me? Living. I couldn't bear the death of the child that was living between us. You never stopped blaming yourself, and it tore us up. But it doesn't have to be that way."

He pulled in under the awning at the hospital. "Be brave, my darling. Be strong for me."

Kat could scarcely stand the pain of his words. Her own life had felt so bleak back in those days. She had barely acknowledged Jake. It hadn't occurred to her he'd been feeling as deeply hurt as she. The same hurt she felt now. She felt doom all around her. Could she be strong?

She had Lilly, but would they ever really be a family? Miss Plum would doubt her suitability as a parent if she didn't show the patience to carry a child to term. If Lilly was gone, would Jake stay? Could her dark side ruin the love they were finding again?

Kat took a deep breath and closed her eyes as she was wheeled to an exam room, trying to calm her racing heart. Jake had put her in a clean gown, which provided some semblance of dignity despite her weakness.

The nurse, brimming with pity, drew her blood until she felt completely drained. Jake sat quietly, holding her hand when he could. His brooding face didn't make her feel any better.

She couldn't understand how he could be so kind to her, even though she felt like she didn't deserve it. What caused the darkness? Her own mother died to give her life. Then her adopted parents died in an accident not long after taking her in. She ruined lives wherever she went.

If she couldn't even keep her own mind stable, how could she ever hope to provide a stable life for Lilly? Her mind was a stormy sea, with thoughts crashing against each other like waves. Crazy as a loon.

Isn't that what Jake used to tell her when they had their famous fights in the travel trailer? And it was true. Maybe that's why she couldn't have babies... shouldn't pass on the crazy genes.

She thought she was done crying when Doc Robbins returned for the last time. His face said it all, and confirmed her fears, but there was a surprise. Her womb only partially failed her.

Jake's shoulders shook as he wept silently, trying to process Doc Robbins's breakdown of her health and the details of her partial miscarriage. While one baby didn't make it, the other twin's healthy vitals were a source of relief. It was unusual, but not unheard of, and her odds of carrying the child to term and surviving increased considerably, the doctor said.

In a few days, Kat would be right as rain.

Kat looked out the window and saw a beautiful sun streaking the sky with the colors of morning. She felt swamped by emotions of loss and hope, leaving her head in a whirl. Sleep overtook her.

Her room was filled with flowers by the time she convinced Jake to leave her and go get her a few things. Doc Robbins had said she'd need to stay two days to watch her insulin levels, but he didn't expect any further harm to her or the baby, because other than being pregnant and diabetic, she was healthy.

They decided to hold off on telling Lilly about the baby until Kat was well enough to come home and show her daughter that she was okay. Then together, they'd tell her what happened.

He would tell Eli and ask him to stay with Lilly again tonight so Jake could stay at the hospital with her. She was glad to be alone for a minute, though. His hovering was driving her nuts.

"Knock, knock," a familiar voice called.

Lana's pregnant frame filled the door, and Kat felt an uncontrolled sob slip through her lips. Lana was someone who understood pain. Her world shattered when they were eighteen, the night her parents bailed her out of jail and were killed in a car accident with her in the back seat. She carried blame like a torch.

"Don't cry, sweet one. It's going to be okay," Lana said, setting a bouquet by her bed.

Kat leaned into her friend's embrace, desperate for the mothering. "I lost one, Lan. What's wrong with me?"

Lana smoothed Kat's hair. "You have type two diabetes, silly. You've always known the risks. That's why you're adopting Lilly. Remember?" She kissed Kat on the forehead, then eased into the chair beside the bed.

"The hardest part here is that you're not off the hook yet. It's up to you to give my little one here a companion that will always be there for them. I know our children will be the best of friends, just like we are, and I can't wait to see it happen."

"I thought I lost them both."

"Kat, honey, you almost died last time. You are being given a gift here. See it for what it is. Accept that your body requires a little extra love, and don't be careless with your life. There are many people who love and admire you."

Lana gestured at the flowers she'd brought amidst the others. "These don't make up for life sucking sometimes, but they bring cheer, if you look for it. You have a lot of love in your life, and you're an inspiration to me, Kat. You never quit when you're determined. Promise not to quit on me, or yourself. Don't go back into that deep hole. You're alive, my dear friend, and you need to focus on that."

She felt the hollow, despite the baby inside. She lost one, and it mattered, and she wasn't ready for lectures. Kat just wanted to grieve for a minute. But she couldn't do it alone. Wouldn't. Not this time.

"I'm alive, but I feel like death. Do you remember the time I told you I was fine growing up without a mom because I didn't know what I was missing?"

Lana nodded and poured a small glass of water from the pitcher next to Kat's bed.

"I lied—I knew. I wanted someone to put my band-aids on for me, explain about my stupid period, and tell me about the birds and bees without using horse anatomy. I wanted to be that person for my children. The mother I aim to be is the one I always wished for growing up. But I'm not sure if I can manage it, because my emotions get so messed up sometimes."

"Don't lie." Lana shook her head. "I've seen you with your daughter. You're a wonderful mother to her and she needs you more than an ordinary child might. She's so much like you. She's still trying to be happy, but I think she's scared it will fall apart. Pull yourself together, Kat, fight for her. Make sure things come together for all of you."

Lana gave Kat a long hug. "I'm done lecturing. I love you."

"You're my best friend, Lan. Thanks for the pep talk." Kat felt marginally better.

"Oh, before I go, I'm about done with you and Jaime avoiding each other. I'm planning Thanksgiving at the Mill and you and Jaime are both coming and bringing your families. You got a little time to set things straight between you two, but if I hear you're hiding under the covers for days, I'll come drag you out myself. Stay tough, okay?"

"Okay." Kat smiled despite herself. She had so many responsibilities and so many more blessings. She could do this.

After two days, she was allowed to leave the hospital and go home, where her family then arranged a small ceremony in memory of the baby they'd lost. Jake wrapped a sheet in a small pine box Eli built, and they buried the box under the ash tree in the backyard. The gesture touched Kat and though she'd put her tears away for another day—they threatened to spill over as Lilly squeezed her hand.

The baby had not developed enough to have a real impact on their lives, but as each person said something, the baby became a little more real to her, and the loss more poignant.

When it was Lilly's turn, Kat's heart broke for the child. Her little girl burst into tears and pulled her hand away.

"This is my fault," she cried, then ran toward the house, long dark braids flapping behind her.

"I'll go after her." Jake tugged his cap around on his head, fidgeting. "I'm just not sure what to say. To either of you."

The last was said so quietly she supposed she wasn't supposed to hear. "I'll talk to her. She has questions only I can answer." She hugged Jake, then Eli.

"Thank you for this... closure. I'll be okay. I'll focus on bringing this one out safely, guys, and I'll take care of me." She squeezed Jake's arm as she passed him to follow Lilly. "Jake, can we talk later?"

He hesitated, and she knew he didn't want to talk about it. Last time, they buried it in silence, which was Jake's way of coping with what he couldn't fix. She was prepared to deal with her heartache alone, but she wanted to give him the chance to heal with her.

She would force herself this time. That little girl needed her. This time, though, she wouldn't make Jake's decision. She had closed him out of her life before because she'd needed to cauterize her pain and that didn't work. She'd do things differently this time.

"We should talk about everything." Jake glanced at Eli. "Can you stay a little while after supper, Eli?"

"It's about time." Eli shook his stick at Kat. "You two better work things out betwixt yourselves so we can focus on working out a plan for Miss Plum."

"Eli, we... Miss Plum?" Kat looked at him, wondering what he was about.

"I have an idea. Invite her to that rodeo of yours, Jake, so she can see how good Lilly is fitting in around here. Kat, you better get to seeing what's vexing that girl before she runs off. It seems to me ya'll generally seem to run off when the going gets tough."

He strode to the stable, muttering to himself.

Kat looked at Jake. "Thank you, I'll be back." She found Lilly sobbing in the corner of her room.

"What is it, honey? Tell me what's bothering you and we'll make it better. Do you have questions about what happened?"

Lilly sniffled, haunted dark chocolate eyes meeting Kat's. Was there something about her that made everyone else miserable? She sat next to Lilly on the floor, picking up a plush pumpkin that had been won at the festival. "Tell me?"

"It's my fault." Her lip quivered pitifully. "I wished I could keep you and Dad all to myself, and then one of the babies died. It should be here, not me."

"Oh, darling." Kat gave her a tight squeeze. "Don't you dare blame yourself."

Her slight frame quivered against Kat, and she smoothed her hair until the sobbing lessened.

"I was just afraid you wouldn't need me anymore. I want to stay here bad, but I didn't mean to..."

Her lip trembled again, and Kat leaned back and used the corner of her flannel to wipe the girl's tears.

"No more of that talk. I'm going to tell you some things about my body that will explain to you the same thing my doctor told me."

Looking at Lilly's earnest expression, she opted for a simple and honest response.

"My sugar levels don't work right for sharing my sugars with the life that was inside me. I was monitoring the sugars, and I was having trouble. One baby is strong, and one was not. There just wasn't enough strength in my body for two babies to grow."

"You seemed fine." Her dubious tone brought a smile to Kat's lips.

"Moms are supposed to be fine. Don't you know I'm really superwoman?"

She was worrying about the problem like a dog with a bone. "Do you think I'll get to stay here? Miss Plum seemed like a mean old lady."

"We don't talk about our elders that way, honey." Kat wanted to scold, but that mirrored her thoughts. She wondered what Eli had up his sleeve. It wasn't likely a woman who didn't approve of paintball guns would approve of the potential of blood and gore at the rodeo.

"Okay. Mom?" Lilly looked at her hopefully. "Can you help me with my school project? My teacher wants me to make a list of ten things I'm thankful for, and all I can think of is my new family and horses."

A laugh barreled out of Kat. "You really are my daughter. What else is there, kiddo?"

Kat rubbed her daughter's thin arms, grateful for the chance to be her mother. "How about you grab a pencil and we'll try to round out that list while we whip up some grub?"

Chapter 15

A bit later, the family had eaten a delicious spread of tacos on fry bread, and Lilly had a list she was proud of. Working together to compile the list reignited Kat's gratitude for the little things.

Besides horses, they discovered a bond in their love of sunrises and sunsets, though Lilly was sure she liked sunrise better because scary things sometimes happened at night. Kat probed, but Lilly seemed unwilling or unable to share, so she didn't push.

They also loved pancakes and pizza, and Jake. Jake had come up so many ways on Lilly's list that it was easy to see how much the kid admired him. She had been adamant that rodeo clowns were on her list at number three—right behind family and horses.

The rodeo was preying on Kat's mind. So many variables. Would Jake get hurt? Is Lug gonna stay sober? Would anyone come, and did she even want to go?

If she allowed Lilly and invited Miss Plum, wasn't disaster inevitable? She had been fidgeting restlessly, driving herself crazy until Jake came up behind her and began gently kneading her shoulders. She surrendered to the treatment and breathed a sigh of contentment.

"You seem tense, babe. Do you want to talk or..."

She sighed. Would they be able to talk, or would they argue? "Eli and Lilly are playing a board game. I thought maybe we could take a walk or a drive..."

"It's a little cool. I'll drive. You have a spot in mind?" Jake pulled his keys out of his jeans and spun them on his finger. "Or should I just drive?"

He looked like he was about to fight a 2000-pound bull while struggling with a red cape. He was worried they'd fight, too.

"How about we just drive down to the landing and park?" Kat asked. "That way, we can turn on the heat if we get cold."

"Sounds like a plan."

As he held out her jacket, she noticed the faint scent of his cologne lingering on the fabric. He fit so snugly into her life. She wondered how she ever thought she could live without him. She slipped into her jacket, then no doubt surprised him by sliding into his arms for a quick embrace.

"Thank you for this," she whispered.

"Don't thank me yet, babe." He held her tightly, then released her. A nervous laugh accompanied the soft look he gave her. "I can't remember one time we've 'talked' about certain things without us going haywire... but, hey, no sense worrying about the bronc you don't have to ride when the one you drew looks mean enough."

As he took her hand, she felt the callouses of his palm against hers and followed him out the kitchen door. When they got parked down at the water's edge, she looked at the setting sun as it created a riot of colorful reflections off the water. She'd always loved the fall.

"Lilly loves sunsets, too, but said scary things sometimes happen at night. Makes me curious about what happened to her."

Jake looked out the window, then rolled it down and let a brisk wind into the cab with them. "We'll just do our best to help her with the future. Scary things do happen at night. Kat, I don't really know if I can talk about this. I thought I could..."

He pulled his ball cap off and threw it on the dash of his truck. Rubbing his hands through his lack of hair, frustrated, he said, "I'm thinking you're gonna just keep doing you..."

"Hold on, cowboy. I think maybe a large part of the problem we've been having the last few years is we're so sure we know what the other thinks we don't wait to hear for ourselves. I know I'm guilty. You've surprised me so much over the past few weeks—I thought you'd split several times, and you held."

"What, I'm going to desert my pregnant wife?" When Jake spoke, his voice vibrated with intensity.

"We didn't even know I was pregnant at first, but yes, I thought you'd find it too much. I thought you would miss the excitement of the arena and you'd be gone, family obligations or not."

"I'm not heartless, Kat."

"Yes, but... you know how it is. There's no since pretending the rodeo doesn't climb inside your head and push rational decisions out of the way in search of glory."

She untwined her braid, using the repetitive motion to calm her nerves. She wished for a way to make this talk simpler.

"It's safe to say that taking my job seriously has always been a part of my work ethic. I won't deny that," Jake said. He fidgeted in the driver's seat. His powerful hands spanned the steering wheel, tracing the emblem with his fingertips.

"After I got stomped, I might have gone a little overboard for a while—"

"A little, Jake? There was betting every night whether you'd be more likely to be picked off by a mean bull or a circuit hottie. You were acting pretty random."

"You wouldn't even talk to me, Kat. My heart was shattered and my spirit crushed, and I realized most of my dad's lessons were worthless if I couldn't ride."

He shook his head angrily, and she let him vent.

"There was a lot going on. You know how much it sucks to stop riding, right? Now you know because of the baby. But it's a new thing, because you've always been crazy about horses. It's like getting your wings clipped. I was afraid coming here would make that even worse. When you heard your horses were in trouble, you rushed back here as fast as you could. You knew I didn't want to come, and it didn't matter enough to ask me."

This was the tipping point, Kat realized. Here is where the shouting would begin and the accusations would fly, all while neglecting the problem—her reproductive system.

She put her hand on his arm and he turned toward her, a wild light dancing in his blue eyes.

"I've done that too often—not ask you what you wanted. I'm sorry for that, Jake. You've always had my back and I appreciate it. How are you taking all this? Do you feel good about what we have now?"

A single tear pooled in the corner of his eye, then he took a deep breath and answered calmly. "I'm unhappy I failed to save you from yourself. My heart goes out to you. Losing a baby hurts, and I mean Melody, too. I'm sorry for not saying that before. It's scary to think we still have two kids to fight for."

She scratched the rough whiskers on his cheek and scooted over to snuggle under his arm as the twilight grew darker.

"I'm sorry about that too, but Lilly helped me to realize no one is to blame. What will be, ya know? I want what we have, not what we've lost. I want you and Lilly, and Eli. And this young one, too, if it's willed."

"Oh babe." His arms tightened around her. "She's a good kid. It's meant to be. She fits right in. I see so much of you in her, and that clown get up, hah, I thought Lug was going to blow a gasket."

"Do you realize she's the same age Melody would have been?"

She felt Jake nod. "The world works in mysterious ways. Does that mean you are going to consider more realistic bedrest? Nothing scares me more than losing you."

"Yes, and after the baby is born, I'm going to ask Doc Robbins to arrange the surgery I should have had years ago. I'm a little on the stubborn side. I won't enjoy being on bed rest, though, and if I get my tubes tied, I won't have to worry about you trying to hogtie me again later."

His warm laughter filled the cab as an owl flew low over the water in front of them. Through his laughter, he said, "Then we'll foster as many more as we can."

She laughed, nestled against his chest, then said seriously, "Are you really going to be okay here, Jake? Honestly, this rodeo thing has got me a bit worked up, but it's only because I care about you. I'm not sure if I'm more worried about you getting hurt in the barrel or disappearing into the circuit, but either way, it's scary."

He tensed. "I can't ride, Kat—"

"Won't," she gently interrupted. "That's another thing that hangs between us, darling. I understand you're afraid—"

"Don't call me a coward. I charge down bulls for a living, err, well, I did. That's not somebody who's afraid."

"That's hiding. You are being as daring as possible on the ground to avoid the possibility of being thrown again, and that's not like you. I never understood why you, of all people, would let a horse beat you. We grew up knowing you had to get back on. I watched you and Jaime with your dad. He's a tough cookie, and he pushed you both to get back in the saddle even though you weren't feeling it. You guys are both tough and strong. I don't get why you didn't try again. You know you're happiest on a horse."

"I'm happiest when I'm with you," he growled.

"I don't want to talk—wait, what if we do just talk about it? That's what you said, right? Fine." Jake took a deep sigh and shifted around a bit. She moved to give him some space, and he growled possessively, pulling her back close against his chest again. Kat felt his heartbeat syncing with hers and she sighed and set in to listen.

"I'm afraid of finding myself under a pair of hooves and maybe not getting up. When I lost my saddle that last time, and then my horse was standing on me, I didn't know if I would stand up again. I guess I got paranoid the tricky critters would win next time. Thank goodness for that rodeo clown who had my back, or I wouldn't be walking around now. What could have happened still gives me nightmares."

"I'll never understand rodeo men—but, you know me," she said, trying to lighten his pain, "if there's a horse involved, I'm for the horse."

"I know, babe. You wanted me to ride, and I let you down." He stroked her arms, causing goosebumps to rise on her skin.

"I had almost proved to myself that I could provide for my family without touching your money. Then you ditched me. It was tough to perform knowing you weren't there. Your lack of interest in me became clear to everyone, and that hurt my pride. I wanted my girl by my side."

This was good. Listening to his story, she realized they'd shared the same feelings side by side, but with a wall of hurt between them.

"When you went back to the life, my initial reaction was hurt, but I decided to be supportive," Kat said. "It wasn't until I saw you lying in the hospital bed that I realized how much I wanted you in my life. Even if you were an insane glory hound. But it was too much. I just couldn't take watching you get knocked around in a barrel by a ticked off hunk of beef. I couldn't watch."

"So, it wasn't because you were ashamed of me, of my job?"

"Jake, I could never be ashamed of you. I was afraid for you. You don't know the meaning of the words too hard. You tackle everything to win. I just wanted you back on your horse where you belonged. You showed an amazing knack for cutting horses from the herd on my ranch growing up, and then you turned it into a career."

She leaned forward and looked back into his twilight darkened features, but he smiled at her, so she settled back and went on.

"I hated to see you give it up because of an accident. You were always so fearless. And the changes you made to accommodate being on foot were not the changes of a man thinking about a family. Then there's me. I don't work that way. I'm always afraid of... messing stuff up, so I have to work stuff out before I do it. Do you know what I mean?"

"There is no more noble a cause than love. None of that matters, because you're the one for me. You're fearless. And there's no one I'd rather be with if I run into a mean snake."

"That's different though," Kat said, "but I love you for saying it." She sat up and turned to hug him in the darkness before sliding back on the seat so she could face him.

"I can commit my time and my money and my smarts, but I never let go of a piece of me. Lilly is possibly the first thing I've ever done that made me feel like I was saying, 'here, this is me, I'll be here for you.' I can give, but giving of myself is different. That should have been you."

"You just weren't brought up that way, kid."

He pulled her back into the comfortable warm spot she'd been enjoying against his side.

"Eli's not exactly a sentimental guy, Kat. You give of yourself generously. Your depth may not be visible to everyone, but that's alright."

She pulled her fingers through her hair, wishing she had her braid to fiddle with. "I cheated you of a satisfying marriage because I couldn't get over myself."

"I don't feel like our marriage was bad," Jake countered. "Sure, it wasn't always perfect, but I know I've been lonely without you these past few years."

"I wasted so much of our time stuck in my head," Kat said, wishing she'd had more clarity.

"It's been enough to know I don't want us to keep going the way we were." She felt Jake shudder. "When you showed up to give me those freakin' papers, I went from being overjoyed that you were back to being terrified of living without you."

"Thank you for coming for me. I had convinced myself that it was time to move on. Even if you were being faithful, there was the constant booty flashing in your face." Kat sighed. "I wondered how you could want to be with me still. I wasn't being a wonderful wife, leaving you out there with no obvious attachment."

"It was hard when you first quit coming," Jake said. "Everyone was talking about how the hero lost his horse and his girl. I won't lie, several girls offered."

He laughed nervously. "It just wasn't what I was about. I had this thing in my head—how being the greatest clown the circuit had ever seen was my ticket to feeling good about myself again. I only realized when you came to divorce me that no job was going to fill the hole in my life left by you."

Her heart fluttered happily. She'd always wondered if Jake was being faithful. She wouldn't have blamed him if he had—hmmm, yeah, she probably would have.

Kat wanted her hero to herself. She grinned in the darkness. "You've always had a silver tongue, Jake. The smartest thing I ever did was marry you before you realized what a neurotic girlfriend I was."

He squeezed her. "What's going on here, Kat? Are we okay? Did we just... talk? And listen?"

She giggled. "Maybe. Yeah. I know I'm supposed to get loud, but I kind of like sitting here, murmuring in the dark. I thought I'd try not to ruin it."

He kissed her on the top of the head, and she felt... good. "So, be honest, are your feet itchy for the arena?"

"In a way..." Jake hesitated. "That first day in the store, I wanted to run. Then you came in looking so hot, and that little boy was holding Lilly's hand and I was like, whoa, somebody has to fend off the boys."

"She is going to be a knockout when she grows up."

"Just like her mama. I didn't think I'd feel better after talking about this stuff, but somehow, I feel like a veil of darkness just lifted from our life and I can hear the freaking birds singing."

"That is birds you hear, dear. The nightbirds are thick."

"Funny girl. I... part of me is wondering now why I didn't saddle back up. What you said about Lug drilling us—that was dead on—but I almost feel like maybe he didn't do it so we could win titles he never did, but maybe, underneath his toughness, he was trying to teach me and Jaime something about life."

"Are you nervous about doing this thing at his ranch?"

Kat remembered how embarrassed both teens had been the last time the Summers ranch sponsored a rodeo. It had been a beautiful day, with tons of people.

It started with Jaime fighting with her mom about how short her shorts could be. Tabby said Jamie couldn't ride in the opening ceremonies because she was being difficult. That made Lug mad, and he got involved, insisting his daughter don jeans as a cowgirl should.

Well, Jaime had her eye on Park Ragland back in those days and she'd been determined to snag him. Jake never liked Park, so he was mad at his sister, but he rarely crossed Jaime. She was the pushier twin.

Unfortunately, Jake didn't ride well when he was mad and his cutting scores were terrible. He failed his roping all together and was so flustered he wouldn't even ride his team roping event.

When Jaime rode barrels, Lug started in on her. Over the loudspeaker. Jake went up to ask his dad to quit being a jerk, and they also announced their argument to the entire arena.

"Are you kidding? Nervous? I mean, which of a thousand things could go wrong? I didn't see another way, though, Kat. My big mouth made promises to the town, and a benefit was the only way I could think of to raise money. It needs to work, because I've already spent it."

He twined her hair around his finger and Kat wished they could sit in the dark forever. "It will work because you're putting it together," she said. "Did you invite your sister to ride?"

"And received a firm no. She's doing good, though. I wish you guys wouldn't be at odds. It's like having my hands not work together." Jake laughed painfully.

"She started it." Jaime's loyalty was in question. "Besides. We don't hate each other or anything. It's just not like it was."

"I'm sorry I came between your friendship."

Kat let out a deep sigh, her breath misting slightly in the cool air. The night was right to share the things that hurt.

"It wasn't you. It was me wallowing in pity about Melody. Jaime is... well, she says what's on her mind and I didn't want to hear it. I felt like she was dumping on me about my selfishness, and I didn't care. I was so angry I wasn't thinking rationally." Kat smiled wryly in the dark. "Thank goodness I'm so much more rational now."

"I wouldn't have you any other way." Chuckling, he squeezed her tight, then released her. He fired up the truck and turned the heater on.

"So, since we can talk without yelling, does that me we can't argue anymore? Because I'll tell you babe, watching you spit nails gets me all fired up, dreaming of make-up sex." He grabbed his hat off the dash and grinned at her as she smacked his arm.

"I make no promises." She rubbed her hands together in front of the heater vent. She hadn't realized she was cold until now.

"What do you think about asking Miss Plum to the rodeo? My gut says it's a bad idea, but I like the thought of trying to repair the damage of the last visit, and seeing Lilly fitting into the community would be a pleasant touch. She did so well on Halloween, I feel confident she can handle it, as long as..."

"I'll manage Lug. He wants Mom back. I convinced him doing this would show his commitment to his family, that he's willing to do what it takes. It's a little sneaky, but I'm planning something last minute to get mom to come."

Kat stayed next to him, but pulled her feet into the truck seat and grinned at him. "You like to live dangerously."

"She was extra smitten with dad back in those days, and I think getting him behind that mic just might give him the courage to talk to her," Jake grinned. "Like really talk, know what I mean?"

"Don't worry, Jake. Things have a way of working out." His earnest eyes were locked onto hers, and Kat felt an overwhelming desire to kiss him.

"Speaking of working out, did Doc mention how long until we can... you know?"

"I'm cleared now, but I'll want to use protection until I can get an operation scheduled." She felt shy. "It's a big decision..."

"It's the right one for us, babe. You and Lilly are the best gals a guy could ask for. Are you okay with it? I'll be by your side."

She leaned back into his arm. "I'm okay with it. I don't want to lose you." She looked at the high moon. "I feel so much better about us, Jake. I've been holding some of that stuff inside so long..."

"So, we're agreed to ask each other what's going on instead of just knowing, right? We'll talk?" She nodded and Jake tugged on the ringlet he'd made of her hair. "So, are you ready to head back?"

"Yeah. Yeah, I am." As he put the vehicle in drive for the short ride back to the house, she asked casually, "So have you got any protection?"

Chapter 16

The morning of the rodeo there was something strange in the air, and it was more than just the warm sunshine after the last week's cooler temperatures. Something was *off*. Kat had a feeling something was going to happen to Jake, but she was worried about sounding like an alarmist if she went on about it.

"C'mon, Mom. I want to get there early so Grandpa Lug can show me his announcer's stuff. He said he'd show me how to work the microphone so I could talk to Dad. I'm so lucky to have two Grandpas." She tugged at her western shirt. "It's way better than none."

Kat looked at Lilly. She felt misty eyed, but she was determined to keep it together. "You look like a perfect cowgirl. I saw you practicing with Eli yesterday. Your barrel racing is looking a lot tighter. Are you sure you want to compete?"

When she'd heard she was going to be allowed to go, she'd begged to take part. Kat thought maybe on the commencement ride or something, but Eli said it was high time for her to be barrel racing. She'd been practicing after school all week. She'd fallen two days ago and Kat raced over, but she dusted it off and climbed back on.

Mr. No Name, the homely appaloosa she'd taken in last month, had taken to Lilly immediately, and the two made a striking pair. He was now YoYo, and he'd added some solid bulk with the extra treats Lilly was always sneaking to him.

The horse was young and a little more spirited than Kat might have liked for her daughter, but the two had forged a bond, and he was perfectly gentle with the girl. She remembered her first horse and there was no way she could deny Lilly her choice.

"For sure. I'm not expecting to win or anything," Lilly said. "I'm just glad to be a part of it." She shook her braid behind her and did a little jig. "Dad says I can't clown around with him since it's too dangerous, but he's going to show me the inside of the barrel. Did you know he has a special trick for getting in quick?"

The pride was clear in her daughter's voice, and Kat prayed things would go well, especially with Miss Plum. Kat had asked Aunt Lucy's opinion, and Lucy seemed to think inviting the older woman to the rodeo was a good idea, as long as everything was safe.

That woman mustn't break up her family...

"Okay, I made sandwiches and put them in the Summer's picnic basket. Will you get the sodas and juices from the bottom of the fridge and put them in the cooler? I've got to make a quick call, then we'll be ready to head over to the arena."

"Okie doke."

Kat watched her daughter dutifully start the task. The child was such a blessing to her. If only... things would be okay. They had to be. Her fainting spells had stopped, and Doc said the babe was doing great.

Jake thought Lug would be okay, too. When he'd come from the ranch yesterday, he'd been in good spirits. He said his dad had gotten a haircut and was wearing new jeans. That was a good sign, but Jake said he was stone cold sober, which was great.

They'd hung signs and made sure the arena was ready, checked all the speakers and had porta potties brought in. Falls Mill was full of travel trailers and the Inn and Out was bursting at the seams with people who had come to town early.

Jake's fan club hadn't suffered with his disappearance. Fans were plentiful. If Jaime had agreed to ride, they might have had to open the Summer's ranch for additional camping. Jaime on a horse was a sight to admire, showcasing her natural talent for horseback riding despite her desire to avoid practice. She'd won a few buckles, and plenty of fans. She'd refused to ride, but promised the boys she'd bring them, so she'd be around.

Kat wished she'd followed up better when Jaime handed her an olive branch this past summer. They'd talked, then gone right back to avoiding each other. Quite a challenge in a small town.

If Kat saw her today, she'd make a point of reaching out.

She dialed Tabby and wondered how this would go. She got to leave a voicemail.

"Hi Tabby, Jake asked me to call and invite you out to the ranch today. He said you'd know you need to be there. We're having a family picnic lunch before the crowds arrive, and we all want you to come."

She took a deep breath and gambled. "Lilly wanted her grandmother to see her ride in her first rodeo, so she especially was asking after you." All true. "Jake said if you were at the store, you should just hang the closed sign and come on down. We hope to see you there."

That done, she and Lilly loaded the coolers and picnic basket, then they led YoYo and Dream, Kat's horse, into the horse trailer. Though she wouldn't be riding, she couldn't leave the old barrel horse behind. She had an idea that Tabby might fancy a ride. Eli came down from the stable loft as they were getting ready to go.

Kat took in her grandfather's appearance and let out a wolf whistle. Lilly looked at Eli in surprise. The weathered old man was gone, a gentleman in his place. Wearing new duds, he'd shined his old boots, his white Stetson was clean, and his long gray hair was bound back in a leather cord.

"Why ya extra gussied up, Grandpa?"

The old man's eyes twinkled as he tweaked the brim of Lilly's hat. "Why, I was planning on keeping Miss Plum company. I figured she'd be more liable to sit with me if I didn't smell like a horse's patoot."

"You like Miss Plum?" Lilly's incredulous voice mirrored Kat's own question. She'd never seen Eli so... cleaned up.

"She seemed a fine enough specimen to me. Can I ride with you ladies? I'll be leaving my horse here today. Reckon I'll leave the riding and roping to the young 'uns. I get enough of that in my day job."

Eli had been doing much of the work himself lately. Kat felt guilty, but Eli was so stubborn. After he ran off Park Ragland, he wouldn't let anyone help him. She was itching to put in more time riding fences, but she was still out of the game for a while. No sense dwelling on it.

"By the by, make sure you get more fuel for that four-wheeler," Eli said. "Jake's been out early and late the last few weeks, stretching that pasture that other cowpoke loused up. I'd hate for the boy to quit afore he got finished, so reckon ya need to keep him in fuel."

"He's almost finished?" She shook her head. All those times, she wondered where he was. She'd just assumed he was working at the Hitchin' Post. "Why didn't I know he was working back there?"

"He said at the rate he was going with everything going on, it might end up being your Christmas present." Eli gave her a sly grin. "He said if you didn't notice, not to mention it. Said you'd rib him about riding a machine instead of a horse. Thought I'd mention it, anyway. So you get the fuel, of course."

Kat thought back, realizing that was what kept tickling her subconscious in the barn. Occasionally, the four-wheeler was out of pocket. Showed how much she cared about the thing.

Jake had noticed it, though, and done her work when she couldn't. Kat swallowed the lump in her throat. She bet that's where he was when he blew her off for that first checkup.

With her man by her side, she could conquer anything. They'd raise their daughter and bring this little one into the world. Not trivial things, but with Jake working with her, they could do it.

Now she had a family to feed. Hopefully Tabby would come.

Regardless, the day would be one for the history books. She still had a feeling in her gut that Jake was in trouble. Her fear existed, but she couldn't resist letting feelings of hope rise to conquer it.

Jake's hip hurt like fire. Lug was getting on his nerves, but at least he was sober. He prayed his mom didn't come. It had been his idea, and he'd worked it all out so they could have a nice family picnic, but being around his dad today made him wonder if his folks really could get along. They were so different.

Maybe he should just leave well enough alone. He'd never been much for meddling in other folks' relationships, so why was he poking this hornets' nest?

"Well, boy." Lug was on a soapbox. "Reckon you've thought this through. I don't mind saying I'm a little nervous. Been out of the box for a spell, but... boy, what I'm trying to say is you haven't been out of the arena, but you've been out of the saddle. Are you sure you don't want to ride today? That Park Ragland's doubtless going to win the cutting, and I know he's been sniffing after your girl. If you beat him, maybe he'll go skulk elsewhere."

Jake wanted to blow a gasket. "I don't want to..."

He stopped. Didn't he? Was he never going to ride again? Watching his daughter work with Eli was bugging him. The old man was missing a few of the important things that turned a rider into a winner. Jake wanted to teach her, but he couldn't do it from the ground.

Jake glanced at his dad's barn. His gear was inside. He'd had it sent here from the hospital, planning for it to rot at this old ranch the same way Lug's was. He knew it was there, because he found his lucky boots in the barn when he needed a confidence boost to go in front of the council.

This was a fundraiser, and he knew they were going to have a big turnout. Maybe he could give them a show. He looked back at Lug. "I don't know if I can, Dad. I think I left my spine in San Antonio."

Lug grinned, a full handlebar mustache making his mouth hard to see, but Jake felt his excitement. "Let's go saddle up

Diego, and see if you got a little left."

"I'm not saying I'll ride. Just saying... I don't know what I'm saying, but let's do it before I change my mind."

Lug clapped him on the shoulder. "Good boy. Can't let a horse get the best of a cowboy. Goes against the code."

Jake leaned his head from side to side, stretching. He was going to do this. Fear fluttered, but he ignored it.

If he got bucked... but this was Diego, his first horse. He was ancient, but Jake wasn't looking for spirit, he was looking for... He grabbed his saddle from the dusty pile of tack, talking gently as he saddled Diego.

Lug just leaned on the doorjamb of the old barn and watched. If there was a horse he could trust, it'd be this one. Once saddled, he turned his back to his dad and spoke gently to Diego.

"We've known each other a long time, old boy. I... If I don't feel quite right up there, give me a minute. I've been out of the saddle a piece."

He stroked the old roan on the nose, noting how much grayer his coat had grown. "We can do this." He took a deep breath and put his foot in the stirrup. "I can do this."

Hooves dancing over his face. Dirt in his mouth. Pain in his hip.

He pushed back. "Sorry, old boy."

He heard Lug snort in disgust from the door, but when he turned to defend his actions, Lug was gone. Jake was done proving himself to the old man, anyway. He'd wanted this for himself—but not bad enough to slide into the saddle again.

Seeing how Diego was ready for the show, Jake led him out to the arena and tied his lead off. He'd ask Lilly to ride him in the closing ceremony so the old boy could get a little taste of glory for his efforts this morning.

Dust billowed up the road, and he was relieved to see Kat's truck and trailer. He wouldn't have to linger on his failure. His daughter's excitement would distract him.

He was glad Kat showed up early, and his grin widened as she wrestled out his mother's picnic basket. Somehow, things had come full circle. Everything was as it should be. He cast a last longing look at Diego and shook his head at himself.

Some other time he'd try again.

"Hi Dad!" Lilly launched herself at him and he swung the six-year-old around like an airplane, delighted by her greeting. "Guess what?" She giggled as her feet hit the ground again. "Grandpa Eli dressed up for Miss Plum. I think he likes her."

Jake did a double take. "Yeah, I'd say he dressed up."

Lug came down from the announcer's stand to greet them and after Kat finished unloading the pair of horses she'd brought, Jake hopped in her truck and backed the trailer out of the way.

He was about to ask Kat how things had gone with his mom when she came up the drive. Kat was stretching out a blanket under the oak tree in the front yard and her face lit up as Tabby got out.

Kat looked at Jake. This was going to go well or blow up.

"I heard my granddaughter was going to ride in this rodeo of yours, Lug, and I had to see for myself that you're up to the task of looking after her."

Tabby crossed the yard, glaring at her husband before pulling Lilly in for an ample hug. "I'm excited for you, honey. Be careful. This sport gets in your head."

Jake wondered who the warning was really for, but it was a fair one. Rodeo had been front and center in the Summers household in their teens, and it kind of replaced their common sense for a while.

"I'm glad you came, Mom." Jake hugged her. "We're going to have a real barn burner."

"I'd guess so, if the traffic in town is any sign. Now I heard we had some lunch to eat. Who is running the concessions, Lug?"

"Kobi from Falls Mill volunteered."

His answer was unsatisfactory, obviously. "Hogwash. She'll never be able to keep up. I'll give her a hand, though. Well, people, are you just going to stand around? Let's get cracking."

Jake grinned at Kat. So far, so good.

If Tabby was happy, things would go smoothly. She was a

pro, having honed her skills over time. Having Lug in the announcer stand and Tabby in the concession stand would make it seem like old times, just hopefully with less family drama.

Lunch went well, although Tabby was done talking to Lug. She ignored him for the rest of the meal, but chatted about racing barrels with Lilly. She'd been a champion in her day and she was enjoying reliving the memories.

Lug was laying back against the tree with his black Stetson pulled over his eyes, but you could tell by the small smile nestled under his mustache that he was enjoying Tabby's stories.

Jake slid up alongside Kat and slipped his arms around her middle. She fought the quick sense of loss his motion gave her and instead settled back into him, letting him hold her. There would be little time for any of them to do anything shortly.

"You have a beautiful family, Mrs. Summers." Jake's husky voice made her middle quiver with lust. They hadn't been able to get enough of each other lately, and Kat was loving every minute of his attention.

"Why, thank you, Mr. Summers." She chuckled, but as she watched her mother-in-law and daughter chatting, she worried. "Do you think it was a good idea to bring Miss Plum out here? What if she disapproves of Lilly riding?"

"Then we'll appeal. It's obvious the kids a natural and we aren't planning to raise her in a bubble just because we didn't give birth to her. She'll be raised the way we decide is best."

Kat straightened and turned to hug Jake. "You're a good man. Please be careful today. I feel..."

"Shhh. Everything's going to be fine. Most importantly, the council's coffers will be full and we can pay for Mrs. Bunsen's new awnings. I got an email from Lana today. She wished us well for the shindig and sent me invoices. Her and Garrett couldn't come out today, but they sent Kobi to help. Lana's such a sweetheart, bless her."

"Nobody better." She was lucky to count the woman as her best friend, but as she looked at her man, and remembered them as kids, Kat realized she was really missing Jaime, snark and all. "Seeing how much happier Lana is with Garrett in her life fills me with joy. It was time for some goodness to come into her life, and she deserved it."

"Ahh, my sweet hearted beauty." Jake kissed her cheek.

She glanced down at herself, suddenly self-conscious. While getting ready, she thought about dressing up to impress Jake's fans, but couldn't find anything better in her closet.

The only thing out of the ordinary today was her belt buckle, which she won in calf roping, of all things. She'd only won one and had never worn it before, but when Lilly found it, she'd insisted. The flannel, jeans, and boots were her go-to attire for any occasion. She was wearing her good hat, too, but she wouldn't call it fancy. Certainly not beautiful.

"She's tough, like you. I've always been glad my sister had friends like you girls growing up."

"Yeah, cuz you were planning to put the make on one of us." Kat grinned, then looked up the driveway toward the road. "Uh-oh. Ready or not, here we go."

A line of trucks and trailers were coming up the road and Jake let out a whoop. "Ladies and gents, today we are going to be amongst rodeo royalty." He smacked Kat on the bottom and ran out to direct the trailers into parking spots on the far side of the arena.

Amid all the hubbub, a compact sedan arrived, and Miss Plum emerged from the car. If Kat hadn't met the woman before, she wouldn't have recognized her.

Gone was the dowdy gray dress and tight bun. She sported blue jeans, turquoise boots, and a purple western shirt. The delicate silver strands of her hair were woven into a loose braid.

Kat double-checked to be certain. The transformation in the woman's appearance was remarkable. Kat signaled to Lilly, and together, they made their way over to greet her.

"Miss Plum, you look amazing. We're so glad you could come out today."

The older ladies eyes were sparkling with excitement, giving her a much softer look. "I'm so glad you invited me. It's for a worthy cause, and besides, I've always wanted to come to one of these things."

She gestured at her boots. "I bought these things years ago, and where do you wear turquoise boots? I've not found the opportunity until now."

Kat gestured at the crowds beginning to mill around, belt buckles and flashy boots abounding. "Well, you're in good company here. Shall we go find a seat, or would you like a tour?"

Miss Plum looked around, then bent to Lilly's height.

"Young lady, let me have a look at you. I can't say I've ever seen a prettier little cowgirl. Tell me, will you ride today?"

Lilly nodded. "Yes, Miss Plum. I'm riding barrels. I'm not very good, but Grandpa Eli's been teaching me."

An extra sparkle glinted in the old gal's eye and Kat thought Eli might have been onto something when he dressed out for her.

"Do you have your own horse?" she asked.

Lilly looked at Kat, wondering if it was okay that she did. Kat thought of Jake's words and nodded. If she didn't approve, at this point it wouldn't matter, anyway. There was no way she was going to tell Lilly she couldn't ride when she'd been working so hard.

"I do. I have an appleoosa... something like that, named YoYo. He's black and white and I love him." Lilly tugged at her braid and Kat grinned, knowing braid tugging was one of her own nervous traits.

"Can I meet him?" Miss Plum straightened, saying to Kat, "I've always loved horses. Never had time for one myself, but I studied up on your ranch. Your work rescuing horses is nothing short of admirable."

She turned to Lilly. "Let me meet your Yoyo." Lilly grabbed her hand and pulled her over to where the horse was tethered.

Kat watched with a smile on her face. This was amazing.

"I could kiss you, Eli."

"Ah, speak of the devil and he'll appear at your side."

"Eli! How did you know she liked horses?"

His weathered face curved into a generous grin. "Never met

me a girl who didn't. And that one, whoo, what a girl. If you'll excuse me, I'm going to go check on Lilly."

He gave her a sly wink and ambled off to where Lilly was showing Miss Plum how she'd woven four strands together to make the braids on Yoyo's mane.

Kat breathed a sigh of relief, feeling a weight lifted from her chest. Now if they could just get through the next few hours without incident... hah! Who was she kidding? This was a rodeo.

Chapter 17

A wave of relief washed over Kat, and she exhaled deeply. Almost done. Lilly had placed fifth in the barrel races. There were only six girls in her age group, but her face was beaming with pleasure and she carried herself with poise.

Jake hadn't been gored to death in the arena, though if it hadn't been for his "special trick" which was just him sliding in and out of the big yellow barrel at lightning speed, he would have been.

Jake signed a ton of autographs... Jaime got cornered for a few, too, though she looked embarrassed. Her two new stepsons looked to be thrilled, though. They were cute little buggers in their boots and jeans. Perfect minis of Tad.

Lug found his groove. He was tickled because the few athletes who wanted his autograph were some of the rising stars in the circuit.

Jake had convinced his buddy Paulo to ride. He'd been earning a lot of points in the standings this season, making him a big draw. He was easy on the eyes, too.

Jake's fan club was shifting. That was fine with Kat. Still, a generous portion of Jake's autographs had gone to females with parts of their anatomy hanging out, but it was all in fun. Occasionally he'd look over and wink at her, or flash her his killer smile.

They were getting ready for the finale. Jake had asked Lilly to ride Diego on the final ride to honor the old stallion, but the girl had yet to lift her butt from the saddle in the last few hours. There were a lot of horses and their riders around the arena, some mounted and some standing, like herself. Kat looked around for Lilly and saw her on her horse inside the arena, talking animatedly with a circle of girls about her age.

The stands were full of all her favorite people, and she saw Vivian holding Ralph's hand. Their resident cougar looked to have been captured. She waved at the Rosati's, and Kendra gave her a thumbs up.

She spied Cynthia and Park Ragland with their heads together, and hoped they weren't up to no good. And since she was feeling charitable, she kinda hoped they fell in love. They deserved each other.

She caught sight of Eli and Miss Plum—or Maddie—as she'd asked to be called, and Eli gave a wave in her direction. Jake was over by the chutes, talking to a few cowboys as they discussed the order the riders would ride in.

Almost done and nothing bad happened.

Looking over at the concession stand, she saw Kobi was doing a great job, which had allowed Tabby to join Lug in the cozy booth.

Jake's parents looked to be getting on better than Kat expected. She figured it was only a matter of time before things blew up, but hopefully, they could patch things up for real this time, since they both clearly loved each other.

She patted Diego on the muzzle and untied him from the ring, heading toward the gate. She would at least walk him in the finale. While the horses were wonderful, the rodeo fever never caught her the way it did the others. Remembering the way Lilly rode, Kat felt sure the girl had been bitten by the bug, but it would be okay. Right now, though, the idea of having her family all to herself soon was what kept Kat going.

Suddenly, there was a loud scream, and Kat's heart skipped a beat. It was Lilly. YoYo reared up, then the horse took off, galloping wildly while Lilly struggled to maintain her grip on the reins.

With lightning speed, Jake jumped onto Diego's back, and they were inside the arena before anyone could react. The horse understood Jake's intent and wasted no time in following his cues. They expertly maneuvered the throngs of people until they were galloping alongside the spooked appaloosa.

Jake pulled Lilly onto his horse, and she nestled into his chest. YoYo's gait slowed down considerably once the rider was gone from his back. He made his way to the fence, his hooves making a gentle clip-clop sound. As soon as Jake and Lilly dismounted, Kat ran to them.

"What happened?" Kat cried. Her heart was racing. Fear had taken over as she'd watched Lilly's wild ride.

And Maddie Plum. That Lilly was in danger would surely have to be reflected in her report, regardless of whether or not Maddie liked horses.

Kat examined Lilly for injuries. "Are you okay, baby?"

"That was a little scary, but I'm good." Lilly was visibly shaken, but a quick inspection revealed she was unhurt.

"What happened? Why did..." Kat rested her head against Lilly as she pulled the girl into a hug.

"We saw the whole thing from over there," Maddie said.

She turned to Jake. "That was quick thinking, young man, and very good riding. Lilly is lucky to have a father like you." She touched Lilly on the shoulder. "Another horse bit YoYo right on the rump. I reckon that would make me jump and run, too. You did some good riding, young lady."

Jake looked dazed, more upset perhaps than Lilly.

"Are you okay?" Kat asked him quietly. "That was huge, Jake. You saved her. On horseback." Jake looked at her a moment, then shook his head, as if to clear the cobwebs.

"Seeing her in danger, I just... reacted. Whoa." He looked around at the hushed crowds, everyone waiting to see if they were okay. YoYo had wandered up and was standing behind Lilly, his head down as if to say he was sorry.

Jake looked at his daughter. "Are you really okay, sugar?"

She nodded, asking, "YoYo's not in trouble, is he?"

With the danger passed, Kat felt a laugh bubbling from her.

This girl was her daughter, no doubt.

Jake nodded. "No, he's not in trouble." He spoke into the mic he used to communicate with the announcer's box. "Mom, Dad, she's fine. Can we get this wrapped up?"

Lug voice came over the loud speaker, where he and Tabby were both on their feet, holding hands, watching with concern. "All right, folks. The young lady is fine. Everyone, mount up. It's time for the last ride. I believe we have a hero out there. Old Diego has earned a spot of honor today, so let's celebrate him as he leads us into the closing ceremony!" A round of applause erupted.

"Do you want to ride with me?" Jake asked Lilly.

She shook her head no. "Can I ride YoYo? He didn't mean to scare me."

Kat shook her head. "I don't think that's a good idea." She looked at Maddie and Eli, who were just watching, and then at Jake. He nodded.

"I think it's a fine idea if your mom agrees. Just to be on the safe side, though, I think you should ride beside me." He looked at Kat shyly, then patted Diego, crooning to the old stallion. "You did great, old boy. We made a great team. What do you say we do it again, a little slower this time?"

Filled with courage that Jake would be close in case... she looked into her daughter's hopeful eyes and looked at Maddie. A slight nod from the old woman cinched the deal, and Lilly saw it in her face.

"Yes!" Her little fist punched into the air as she turned to climb on YoYo's back. "Dad, can you give me a boost?"

"Jake, I got to hand it to you." Weeks later, Sheriff Tate was holding his hat. Behind him, Main Street almost glistened. "I didn't think you had it in you, but..." He shuffled his feet, obviously uncomfortable. "It seems like you aren't the bad apple, I thought. Mrs. Bunsen has been crowing about the new awnings, and well, the town just looks spruced up. I'm supposed to ask if you would consider joining the council since you raised so much money and all."

Jake's jaw nearly hit the floor.

Speaking of floor, he realized Lilly and her friend Kevin were doing an excellent job of keeping the floor swept. The traffic in his store the last month had been heavy, and everyone had a place to be and a job to do, something old Hank had done for him once. The kids were crushing it.

When he bought the Hitchin' Post, he'd been trying to get closer to Kat, maybe find something to do in this boring town. Glancing around him, he realized he'd made his place.

Then he shifted his attention to Sheriff Tate's sizable frame, and he realized he had accomplished even more. He'd become a part of the community.

He shook his head. "No, Sheriff, that kind of interfering ain't for me. I made a big enough stir just trying to get a few things accomplished. I think I'll rein my act in here at the store. Leave the big decisions to folks more qualified."

"Well, tarnation, Jake. Ain't nobody qualified til they work at it. We could use your kind of energy around here."

Jake gestured at the western clothing section. A woman and her two children were selecting Christmas presents, and the sight of their pile made Jake's pocket happy.

"I'm using my energy here, and any I have left over, I'm saving to get into mischief. I wouldn't want you to think any more of me, Sheriff." He winked at the man's surprised face. "Now, unless you're needing a new ax handle..."

"I don't need a—hey! Who told you I needed a new handle for that dad burned tool?"

"I heard you had a run in with a tough tree and it got the best of... your ax." Jake laughed. "It's a small town."

"Well, maybe with what you kids have started around here, we might grow instead of becoming a bygone of the past. I heard Garrett Wilcox was adding horseback riding into his resort plans. He was in registering permits a few weeks ago. Maybe he'll bring that girl of yours some business. I heard he was interested in her horses."

"Well, I'll pass that on." Had he known that? "Now, Sheriff, about the ax handle?"

"I'll take two." He growled at Jake, but it was clearly in annoyance at the tree. "That durned red oak wouldn't bust for nothing and I maybe let my temper get the best of me."

Jake selected two handles from a bin and rang them up. "Happens to the best of 'em." He shuffled around, leaning against the counter. "By the way, I'm planning on a little more expansion on my tack, so if you think I ought to talk to Lug about—"

"Do it. The rodeo was good for this town. I know your pa has a hankering to bring back the family rodeo. Your dad is not a bad guy, he just—"

"No worries, Sheriff. I got a bead on my pa. It's my ma I worry about."

A light shimmered in Tate's eyes as he leaned in, about to impart juicy gossip, no doubt. "Kobi let on Lug took Tabby to dinner at Falls Mill last night, and they stayed a mighty long time."

That was news, good news even, but none of his business. Gossip would never be his thing. "Well, folks gotta eat, ya know. Speaking of," Jake looked pointedly at the family coming to check out, "I've got plans, so I'll be tending my customers and heading out."

After accepting his friendly handshake, Jake knew Sheriff Tate was sewed up. He wouldn't need to take any more guff from him. With a wry smile and two new handles, the Sheriff headed for the door.

"Think about the council. We could use some young blood."

Jake smiled, not even tempted. Keeping the store up and his women happy was all the challenge he cared for. He had a clear vision of the future and knew this business would be his legacy if he stayed on course. Maybe something he could pass on to one of his kids, he thought with a grin.

It was a good feeling, being counted on. He rang up his customers cheerfully and gave a last long look around before locking up for the night.

This was right.

The sun was setting as he drove to the ranch, his stomach

growling in anticipation of the meal to come. They were celebrating a Thanksgiving feast early because Kat's Aunt Lucy was coming from St. Louis.

It surprised him to see Maddie Plum's car when he pulled in. They stepped out at the same time.

"I wanted to talk to you, young man. I'm feeling a bit like some holiday magic, so I twisted a few arms to get this paperwork pushed through. Lucy told me you were having dinner today, so I wanted to get these here."

Maddie handed him the adoption papers. "All that's required is your signatures and then I can file them and Lilly will officially be your daughter. Lucy suggested I talk to you first. Shall we go tell everyone?"

Jake thought, clutching the papers as if they were gold plated. "I have an idea. If you'll come in, Maddie, but not mention it yet. I think Lilly would like to give the papers to Kat."

"Magic, I knew it. When I first saw you, I thought... well, I'm glad I thought wrong. I love it when I get to bring a family together. It makes my job worth doing."

Jake tucked the papers in his back pocket and escorted Maddie to the kitchen door. The scene inside warmed his heart as females bustled around the kitchen wearing aprons and flour. Lilly was wearing a chef's hat and filling deviled eggs.

"Look who I found. Another guest for our glorious feast." A chorus of greetings ensued, though Jake noticed the cautious look in his wife's eyes and the excited look in Eli's.

The man was smitten.

He winked at his wife to reassure her, but he wasn't sure it worked. Another place was laid for Maddie, and their warm chatter filled the room. When Kat started whipping the mashed potatoes, Jake spirited Lilly from the room.

"Heya, sport. Guess what Miss Maddie brought?" Jake looked at the adorable elf that was almost officially their daughter.

"What?"

He pulled the papers from his back pocket and grabbed a pen off the coffee table. "These papers say you can stay with us forever. I know your mom wants that, so that just leaves me and you. I've decided to stay, kiddo, and be your forever dad if you'll have me. How about you, Lilly, planning to stay with us for the long haul?"

"Please." Tears filled her eyes, and she ran into his arms.

"Hey, don't cry. This is a happy time." Jake was wondering if his plan backfired. Tears were not what he expected, then he realized his own were threatening to spill.

"I'm happy. These are happy tears. Can we go tell Mom?" Lilly wiped her eyes.

"Yup. Let's go tell her. Hold on." He scrawled his name next to the word Father.

This was right.

"Would you like to do the honors, Lilly bear?"

She nodded, carefully accepting the pen and papers, and pushed through the kitchen door to where Kat was stirring gravy in a cast-iron skillet.

Jake looked at the gravy and the look on Kat's face as their daughter held the pen out. He'd have to keep an eye on that gravy once Kat started crying her happy tears.

The knot in his throat had loosened, but barely.

"Miss Maddie says I can be your forever daughter. If you're sure."

Her voice quivered, and Jake got a sense of just how uncertain her life had been—til now. He knew it wouldn't be the last time insecurity struck his daughter, but he knew it was the last time she'd have to feel it alone.

Now she'd have her family beside her.

Kat looked at the miracle standing before her. The moment Maddie stepped through the door, Kat's intuition told her that something serious had happened. Things had been going far too well, so she'd suspected the worst. But this wasn't bad. This was her daughter, holding out her adoption papers.

She knelt down, looking into dark, hopeful eyes. "I know you've had a tough time, Lilly, but that is over. I say yes! We have a connection as tight as any family. This news has me over the moon!"

She took the papers and noticed Jake had already signed. Her heart bounced. He had truly committed. She looked at Jake and he winked at her as he moved to stir her gravy.

"We are a family. Even if Miss Maddie hadn't wanted me to stay, you would have found a way to keep me. I knew you were meant to be my mom. I can't believe I also got a dad and grandpa. Two grandpas... and Grandma Tabby. Anyway. I don't wanna leave. I wanna stay with you. I'm sorry about... about the baby, but I'm glad you have enough love for all of us. I wanna be like you when I'm grown up."

Lilly tugged on her ponytail, and Kat laughed through the tears streaming down her cheeks. And she thought she wasn't a crier. Despite the teardrops hitting the paper, they were happy tears, so it was surely okay.

She signed next to Mother, then passed the papers back to Maddie, who looked suspiciously like she was hiding some happy tears of her own.

"By the way, Mom?"

Kat wiped her cheeks and looked at her daughter, the most precious sight in the entire world.

"Yes, honey?"

"After the baby comes, if you still have a lot of hugs like now, can you have Aunt Lucy find me a big brother? I like hugs, but I have a feeling me and the baby are going to need someone else to help share all the love. You and Dad should think on it."

She walked to the table and sat down between Maddie and Lucy. "Now I'm hungry. Dad, can you bring the gravy? Let's all stop crying so Grandpa Eli can say grace."

Kat laughed as she put her tears away for good. Setting the turkey platter on the table, she smiled as Jake walked past the empty gravy boat and set the pan in the middle of the table. It sat on the ring that had been burned into the wood a long time ago.

Kat wondered if her own dad might have put gravy there while her mom watched patiently. Those things she missed with her own mother, she would have with Lilly. She looked at Lucy, and the knowing look in her aunt's eye told Kat her family wasn't done growing yet.

Eli said grace and when he said he was grateful Lilly had come into their lives, Kat knew without a doubt, it was the happiest day of her life.

Later that night, the dishes were washed, and the company was bedded down or seen off, and Jake lay next to Kat in their bed, twining her hair around his finger.

"You really did it. If you would have told me three months ago that the whirlwind of our lives would take us down the route it did, I wouldn't have believed it. I should've just trusted. Kat, with you, life is always a wild ride."

"Speaking of riding, Jake, now that you ride again, are you still okay with choosing this life? I don't want a rodeo life for Lilly, but I can tell it's going to be hard to talk her down. I mean, I'm not saying we could come to all your events, but she's old enough we could travel to the closer ones..."

"I love you for saying that, but I'm not aiming to leave my family behind. I want more for you girls, and whoever this little one is." He drew a heart on her belly with his finger.

Kat snuggled closer to his lean frame, warmed as much by his warm body as she was by his words. She wouldn't have to give him up again. This was the best day of her life. Her daughter and her husband, both hers.

"I have to tell you, though, I was talking to the Sheriff, and he agreed the town needs a rodeo. Not some big show like this last one, just good family fun, like the old days. Something that caters to the youngsters and old timers. Like me."

"That's great. A throwback to the old days, huh? What you've done for this town already, I can't believe you did it, but it's awesome. You gave people confidence. Do you know what I saw on Main Street? Shoppers. Go figure."

She hesitated. "The rodeo... will you..." The idea of him clowning scared her, but he was great at it, so she'd have to trust him the way he trusted her.

"Will I ride? Heck yeah. I wasted too much time in a barrel when I belong on a horse. You were right."

"I had nothing to do with that. You just... rode when you needed to."

"You had everything to do with it. If it weren't for you, always pushing me to talk about feelings, I'd still be bottled up like a bad genie."

Kat giggled and snuggled deeper. "All right, bad genie." She rubbed his bare tummy briskly. "I already got my first and second wish." She whispered in his ear, and he gave her a mischievous grin. "If you can do that, all my wishes will have come true."

One Year Later

Kat and Jaime exchanged a knowing smile as they sat on the porch, watching the children take on the men in a spirited game of whiffleball.

Lana pushed out the heavy wooden door of the restaurant, which was closed for the holiday, but was hosting what they'd decided last year needed to be an annual Friendsgiving.

"This feels right," Lana said, a golden-haired sleeping cherub on her hip. Kat gazed at her two closest friends, who were beaming at the small bundle in her arms. She realized that this past year had been an unforgettable journey.

"I'm so glad you and my brother finally got your act together," Jamie said. "It was a long time coming, but I love the life you've carved out for yourselves."

"Look who's talking?" Kat teased. "You've come a long way from moving every three months. You've been married for over a year." She covered the mirth in her voice, but Jaime grinned knowingly. "Congratulations on that awesomeness. I'm so glad we're all here, dear friends."

"I'm glad too, Kat." Jaime picked up a photo off the stack of photo albums Kat brought. It was a shot of the four of them as teenagers on Halloween when they were Ghostbusters. "I missed a lot of things, including your incessant picture taking, but you've definitely gotten back into the swing of things, for which I'm grateful."

Kat grimaced. "Uhm, hey, I think I need to take this one for a diaper change. Make sure those goons stick to easy tags, or the kids will be hanging on them, and they'll get all scuffed up before we do pictures."

"Yes, Mom," Jaime teased. "And hey—Jaime motioned for Kat to hand her the baby. "I'll take one for the team. Hand me the little darlin' and I'll change her. I skipped diapers and shot straight into T-Ball, so I can use my niece here to remind me why I never want to start from scratch."

She was totally serious, and they all cracked up. Kat carefully passed sweet little Hope to Jaime and sank back into the rocking chair, breathing out a content sigh. Lana expertly slipped her own little one into her lap and reached out to squeeze Kat's hand.

With a hint of nostalgia in her voice, Lana said, "I never imagined life could be this wonderful. Having both of my best friends by my side while I juggled everything this past year has been an invaluable blessing."

"You guys adopting a dozen horses saved my hide, sweet cheeks," said Kat, "I owe you big."

"We just had so many requests for trail rides, it seemed like a perfect solution. I've just been so busy..." Lana shrugged.

"I've just been sitting on my rump out here," Kat said. "Did you need help in the kitchen?"

"I cheated," Lana giggled. "Today, I hired Kobi to cook."

Kat's eyes lingered on the old mill, her mind flooded with memories of the games they played as kids in a building that was now part of a luxury resort complex.

"I think Kobi's decided for sure to stay on and manage the back of the restaurant for us," Lana confided. "She might have her eye on the contractor Garrett's been working with, but there's no telling. She's pretty dedicated to learning."

"You guys sure lucked out with her."

"Well, when I was pretty sure family had permanently filled Jamie's time, I offered Kobi a hefty salary, and she's worth every penny." Lana shifted the baby around carefully, then winked at her, and glanced up the road. "So yeah, she should have our spread laid out in about twenty. When Jaime gets back, shall we gather up our clan for pictures?"

Kat thought it sounded perfect. Everything was right. Just then, there were Indian whoops from the boys, and several more cars drove into the parking lot. Lana grinned.

"Right on time," she said.

Upon seeing them, Kat's eyebrows shot up in surprise. "What's this?"

"Well, since I was cheating already, having it catered, and we have the restaurant to ourselves, I figured we'd enjoy an ownership perk and invite the rest of our families," Lana said with a smile.

She wasn't kidding. Grandpa Eli helped Maddie out of her car, and Eli's dog, Lucky, had apparently hitched a ride as well. He made a beeline to sniff Tad's dog, Hydro, then the two hounds were bouncing around the children like old friends.

Watching the melee with amusement for a moment, Eli turned his gaze to Maddie, his eyes softening as he took her hand. Jasper and Emily joined them, and Jasper said something funny to Eli, and Emily just rolled her eyes and introduced herself to Maddie.

Tabby started hollering and laughing from the third new rig. Lug was dropping the truck's tailgate for his old red boned hound, and Tabby needed him to carry pies.

After giving the old dog a good pat, the dog's tail wagged happily as he made his way up to the porch of the restaurant, where he lay down contentedly by the door. Tabby handed out several pies from the cab of his truck to Lug, who was grinning from ear to ear.

"I told her I had everything covered, but she said she gets huge amounts of followers on her social media when she posts pictures of herself baking." Lana giggled, shifting her little boy as he started to wake up from all the new commotion. "I looked, and she's not lying. I never thought the twin's mother would fancy herself an influencer, but she definitely had an influence on us over time, didn't she?

"Each of us seeks outdoor magic," Kat said. "That's one gift from her."

"And we all speak our mind, us four that she took under her wing," Lana added.

Jaime stepped out, holding Hope close. "And she taught us all that with a little home cooking packed in a picnic basket, we can achieve our hearts' desire."

They laughed while the newcomers collected hugs from down where the men, kids, and dogs were playing. "Did you guys know she has a social following of people who watch her bake pies?"

The girls shared a look and then burst into giggles.

Jaime was still holding Hope, and she and Lana carried the babies to the greetings. Kat picked up her camera to capture the moment. Her heart was overflowing with emotions as she watched Lilly with Cal and Ry—Tad and Jaime's boys—and it was good to see her playing with friends.

Kat snapped a picture of Lilly with her arms around both boys, just hanging between them, and all three just grinning like gooses.

She'd treasure it always.

Everyone tolerated several minutes of smart phones flashing. While Kat took her pictures, Tabby and Maddie did, too.

"All right guys," Kat said, "let's head in for our Friendsgiving feast that our favorite host has had prepared for us."

She winked at Lilly. "The amazing Kobi will be our chef."

Lilly fist pumped the air and told Cal confidently, "Totally order the chicken nuggets. Kobi makes the best. And get the orange sauce, trust me."

Kat loved this little lady of hers. Lilly was scooped up alongside the grandparents with the other kiddos as Lana started herding everyone in.

Somehow Jaime ended up with Hope again, so Kat was empty-handed when Jake caught her arm and held her back.

"Hey, I think we have more guests coming, but I need to ask you something before they get here." Jake looked relaxed, so she wasn't sure why his tone was so intense.

"Yeah, hit me with it, hon." She started to walk, but he halted her.

"Your Aunt Lucy is coming. She called a bit ago. Eli gave me the message, but he said it was urgent, so I called her back. She hit me with a question I wasn't sure how to answer."

Kat was curious, but reckoned why not with so many extra guests? "It will be wonderful to see her. What's the question?" Kat paused. "And who is with her?"

"Well, that's kind of the question. She was headed this way to pick up a young man about ten years old who recently landed in the system. She plans to keep him until he can be placed in a foster home. Incidentally, I asked her how hard it was to get approved to foster, and she suggested we talk to Maddie."

He took off his hat, scrubbing his hand through the caramel curls that had grown back this last year, before snugging the hat back on.

"I asked her to come and bring him, since they'd be nearly here anywhere. I figured it'd be cool with Lana... What I mean to ask is I know we're crazy busy, but do you think we might be able to clear some space for another kiddo who might need us?"

Kat was stunned. She heard gravel crunching up the road.

"Look," he said, "I asked her not to say anything to him—Jared's his name—he thinks he's just along for the ride with a brief stop for some grub, so there's no pressure. I knew this was something we needed to talk about, decide together."

"Wait, Jake, this is amazing. I love your heart." Kat kissed his cheek, and then waved at Aunt Lucy's car as it pulled into a parking space.

"How very handy that Lana invited Maddy." Kat grinned. "We'll talk to her about applying to foster and see where it goes from there. In case I haven't told you today, husband, I love being your girl."

Jared was shy, and he looked uncomfortable, but Jake took him under his wing, and the boys went inside, leaving her and her aunt to follow.

"Did Jake have a chance to talk to you?" Lucy asked.

"He did, and I think we are going to talk to Maddie." With

a lightness in her step, she added, "I think we are both in love with the idea. And I suspect Eli and Lilly will approve. She asks now and then about a brother since she got a sister."

"Good news," Lucy said. "Let's get in there so I can get some hugs and see that new baby. I love this time of year. Good things happen."

When they walked in, the scene was nothing short of a holiday miracle, the four friends and their families all sharing love and cheer in the dining room as they found seats at the two long tables covered in food.

Lilly waved at her, excited. "Hey Mom, I want you to meet Jared. He's ten, and he's going to live with Aunt Lucy for a while, just like I did."

Just like Kat did. So many of life's little connections that would go on to create these big connections. As she looked at all of her family in the room, it truly surprised her at how much it had grown.

"So, Jared, what grade are you in?" Kat asked.

He looked at her shyly and ducked his head. "I'm in fifth. They might hold me back since I missed some school this year, so I don't know."

"It's never too late," Lilly said. "Maybe I could help you with some catch up work."

With a knowing smile, Kat said, "We never know what the future holds, darlin.' Now let's fix our plates." Jake appeared beside her and pulled out her chair, and Jaime, holding Hope, quickly slid into the chair he'd picked for himself.

"Too slow," Jaime taunted her twin. Jaime looked at Kat. "I'll hold Hope while you eat, okay. Then we'll switch."

Kat smiled at her gratefully. "You don't know how much that's worth, sis."

"Well, truth be told, I'm smitten with this little angel, so it's mostly just me being greedy, but you're welcome."

Tabby swung by and scooped Hope out of Jamie's arms. "Nonsense, you girls eat. I'll hold the baby."

Lana's little man threw mashed potatoes at his high chair, and a big hunk flew across the table and hit Lilly on the arm.

She quickly licked off the blob and told Jared she recommended the chicken nuggets *and* the mashed potatoes. The children's laughter echoed through the room, punctuated by requests for mashed potatoes.

Jake was still standing behind Kat's chair, behind her and Lilly and his sister, and he leaned down and whispered in her ear. "Does it get any more perfect than this?"

Lilly spoke up, and said, "Of course it does, Dad. These grown-ups need more kids to hug." With a hopeful expression, she turned to Jared and asked, "Is there any chance you could stay with us?"

Lilly looked up at Kat and Jake with serious eyes. "Mom, Dad, you guys think about it."

Kat and Jake laughed in harmony, then shared their special smiles with Lucy and Maddie.

"What lies ahead is a mystery, Lilly," Jake said. "But this family's got what it takes, so the future's looking right and bright."

Jared looked around shyly for a second, but when Jake nodded encouragingly at him, he relaxed, and asked, "Can someone pass the mashed potatoes?"

Jake nodded and reached over Kat for the bowl to hand over. "Yes, sir, a man after my own heart."

A warm sense of satisfaction enveloped Kat as she saw the delight on the faces of her family and friends. All her dreams came true.

Would you love to hear all three stories in the Riverbend Falls series narrated for your listening pleasure?

Audio Releases Coming in 2024

Lana's Leap

Planting Jasmine

Keeping Kat

Books written by Delilah Dewey

Published by Delilah's Diction

adelilah@delilahsdiction.com
www.delilahsdiction.com

About the Author

Delilah Dewey spends her small hours of the morning crafting genuine tales of small town romance, before leaving for her fulfilling day job as a Trust department secretary. She loves to immerse herself in the research process, exploring every detail.

When she isn't working at a computer, or spending quality time with her own romantic hero, she can be found cuddled up to a book, soaking up the warmth of the season, or donning her boots and gloves and tackling whatever tasks present themselves.

Delilah loves outdoor activities, like camping in a tent near the river, admiring the wildlife, and enjoying a warm campfire in the evening.

Visit Delilah's Author Page on

Facebook or Amazon,

and check out her website at

delilahsdiction.com